Speechless in New York

Ellen Dreyer

FOUR CORNERS PUBLISHING CO.
NEW YORK

Four Corners Publishing Company
45 West 10th Street, Suite 4J, New York, NY 10011

Printed in U.S.A.

Cover illustration by Catherine Huerta
Maps by Compass Projections, Anita Karl and Jim Kemp

03 04 02 01 00   5 4 3 2 1

Library of Congress Cataloging-in-Publication Data

Dreyer, Ellen.
Speechless in New York / Ellen Dreyer. -- 1st ed.
p. cm. -- (Going To)
SUMMARY: Members of the Prairie Youth Chorale fly from Chicago to New York City to sing at a youth chorus festival in this story with an appended nonfiction guide to sites of interest to school children.
ISBN: 1-893577-01-5
1. New York (N.Y.)--Juvenile fiction. 2. Children's choirs--Juvenile fiction. 3. School children--Illinois--Travel--Juvenile fiction. 4. New York (N.Y.)--Description and travel--Juvenile literature. I. Title.

PZ7.D78395Sp 2000   [Fic]
QB199-1002

Lovingly dedicated to my parents,

Harvey and Doris Dreyer—

two true New Yorkers.

CONTENTS

CHAPTER ONE

A Dream Come True?

"Look, we're right over the Statue of Liberty!" someone shouted from the back of the plane.

Jessie Witt pushed her curly brown hair out of her eyes. She leaned across the girl next to her, Chi, to gaze out the window, long enough to see a tiny, glowing speck in the harbor below. It looked pretty in the late June afternoon light.

The symbol of freedom, she thought. It fit her frame of mind. She'd arrived at the city where singers made it big. As maybe she would someday. This was the place she'd wanted to visit for years. *Nothing* was going to get in the way of her having the time of her life.

When the plane finally touched down, tires squealing on the runway, Jessie cheered along with many of the other passengers. A few minutes later, all twenty-five in Jessie's group—select members of the PYC, or Prairie Youth Chorale, here in New York to sing at a youth chorus festival—headed down the corridor in La Guardia Airport toward the baggage claim. She was glad to be off the plane.

Something in that stale air had been making her cough almost all the way from Chicago.

"La Guardia, isn't that something you can get from the water?" a familiar voice joked.

Jessie glanced at Mike Ribert, who'd obviously hurried to catch up with her. She couldn't imagine why.

"No, Ribbet," she shot back, "it's a disease you get from never keeping your mouth shut."

"Ha, ha," he retorted. Then, in a quieter voice he added, "Do me a favor? Don't call me Ribbet." He walked swiftly away from her.

Jessie realized all of a sudden that she had hardly said one word to Mike all year, even though they were from the same school and had several classes together. From fourth grade all the way till the end of seventh, he had teased her every chance he got. A day without some silly comment or joke at her expense from "Ribbet" (one way she'd learned to fight back was to give him this froggy nickname) usually meant he was out sick.

But all that seemed like long ago. She felt tongue-tied as she rode down an escalator surrounded by the excited chatter of the other PYC-ers and entered the baggage claim area. *It isn't as if you're buddies with anyone in the group,* she reminded herself. True, she'd been singing with them for the past few months. But only two other kids besides Mike came from her school. The rest were from five other junior and senior highs scattered all over the Twin Cities of

Minneapolis and St. Paul. She couldn't possibly get to know all of them.

Besides, making friends quickly had never been her forte.

Carousel A was designated for their flight. Mr. J. (for Jacobs), their music director, waved them toward the end of the belt nearest where the luggage came out. Some other passengers from the plane seemed disgruntled as they moved away to make room for the large group. Jessie found herself standing near enough to Mike to take another look at him. He must have sprouted about a foot since seventh grade, and he was, she had to admit, somewhat cute, with longish black hair that spilled over his shirt collar and eyes that looked bluer than she remembered. Then his face turned toward her, and she quickly looked away as Kendra Roberts walked up to Mike and set down her two overstuffed carry-on bags. One of them, Jessie knew, was filled with makeup. Kendra had spent the whole hour of the Chicago layover putting on her face in the ladies' room. At fifteen, she was one of the older kids in the choir, and by far the best soprano. She'd made it clear on every possible occasion that she was going to become an opera singer.

"Have you seen my suitcase?" she asked Mike, tossing her sleek cornrows over her shoulder. The gold beads at the end of each one clacked noisily.

"No. I have no idea what it looks like," Mike answered.

"You know," Kendra replied, in a sing-song voice, "it's the one with all the stickers on it, from all the places I've traveled."

Jessie turned away, rolling her eyes. Kendra had everything she needed to become an opera diva, she thought—including an ego the size of North America.

"Oh, no!" someone cried out. Chi pushed forward until she was right beside the belt. Her small frame exuded nervous tension. Jessie stood on tiptoes and saw a pink, hard-sided suitcase coming around the bend, open, its contents spilling out between thick pieces of tape: a pair of jeans, a nightshirt, a mashed paperback, and a green stuffed animal. Jessie watched another girl, named Vicky, help Chi drag the damaged suitcase through the thick cluster of kids. Chi's eyes were filled with tears. *What bad luck,* Jessie thought, hoping her own suitcase had arrived intact.

Only two other kids were still standing at the belt, waiting for their luggage: Kendra and Justin O'Malley, a seventh grader whose round, freckled face was deceptively innocent looking. One lonely suitcase was going around and around.

"I need my suitcase," Kendra went on, her voice growing louder and more agitated. "It's got my concert outfit in it. And my Juilliard application."

"Juilliard?" Jessie blurted, turning to stare at Kendra.

"Of course. I want to go there, and I can get in."

At fifteen? Jessie wondered. It was a wild possibility, though she had to admit, part of her was envious of Kendra's self-confidence.

Just then Mr. J. came rushing out of a small office next to the baggage carousel. His salt-and-pepper hair was unusually ruffled.

"Guys," he said, frowning owlishly as he waved a bunch of printed forms overhead, "I have some bad news for you." He handed a form to each of them. "Please fill these out. Your bags got on the wrong flight."

"No!" Justin cried out, melodramatically pretending to topple off the belt.

With a sigh, Jessie took the form and joined the other two at a nearby counter to fill it out. There were photos of various kinds of suitcases all over it. She circled the one that looked closest to hers.

"I can't believe this," Jessie mumbled. Suddenly she started coughing again and had to take a drink from her water bottle. "What are we going to do if we can't get them back?"

"Go on a massive shopping spree," Kendra said.

With a snort, Jessie tried to concentrate on the form. She failed. "Some of us don't have that kind of spending money," she muttered.

"Don't you have a credit card?" Kendra replied incredulously. "*All* parents should give their kids plastic in case of emergencies."

Fixing her eyes on Kendra, who was signing the form with an elaborate signature, Jessie decided that she would simply ignore whatever the budding diva said from now on.

She had to list the contents of her suitcase. That was easy enough. It had taken so long to pack that she'd memorized every item. For all she knew, someone in Australia would be enjoying her favorite sling-back sandals and cutoff shorts, not to mention what she was supposed to wear to sing on Wednesday: the long black skirt, lace-trimmed white blouse, and red bow tie flecked with gold stars. And what about the gifts for her aunt, uncle, and cousin that her mother had packed in her suitcase? Would she have to shop for presents for her New York family, too?

Unfortunately, Mr. J. did nothing to lessen her fears. When he reemerged from the lost-luggage office after having submitted their forms, he still wore a grim frown. “Well,” he told them, “I have some good news and some bad news. It seems they’ve located your bags, Kendra and Justin, on a flight to Dayton, Ohio. The other one—” he turned to Jessie—“hasn’t been found yet.”

All the air went out of Jessie’s lungs. She felt as if someone had just punched her in the stomach. The next breath she took led right into an uncontrollable fit of coughing. Mr. J. patted her back.

“Jessie, Jessie, are you okay?” he asked.

“She’s just bawling,” Kendra said.

“I am not,” Jessie started to reply, just as her vision grew blurry with tears…big, fat, cough-induced tears.

Her dream trip was turning into a nightmare!

CHAPTER TWO

I'll Take Manhattan

About a half hour later, the airport shuttle bus arrived in Manhattan, maneuvering through streets crowded with honking taxis and cars, big trucks and cyclists. There were floods of pedestrians on the sidewalks, and at each corner they even crossed the street against the light. Jessie, who'd been feeling morose and preoccupied with her lost bag, Kendra's mean words, and her strange exchange with Mike, was jolted out of her thoughts by the amazing sights going past her window.

Tall buildings rose up on either side of the street, blocking out the sun and making her feel as if she were in a canyon. How did people stand to live so close together? And Manhattan was only one borough, or city-within-a-city, in New York. There were also Queens, Brooklyn, the Bronx, and Staten Island. Just thinking about the sheer physical size of this city was overwhelming. It made Edina, Minnesota, where she had lived her whole life, look like a one-horse town.

The streets grew more and more crowded the further south they drove down Fifth Avenue. When Central Park appeared on Jessie's right, it was a relief to her to see so much green and so many flowering trees just over the park wall. She also saw people riding horseback, kids playing in a playground, a hot-dog vendor's cart. Even though she could barely see into the park through the June foliage, she knew from looking at her map that it was enormous. Like everything else here seemed to be.

Finally they crossed the park and ended up on the Upper West Side. Their hotel, the Milburn, was sandwiched between rows of apartment houses on West Seventy-sixth Street. It looked reasonably small, but it was a lot more elegant than the budget family motels Jessie had been to in the past.

"I can't believe this humidity!" someone remarked.

"Just wait," someone else answered. "It's going up into the nineties this weekend."

Chi stepped out in front of the group with her camera. Before she could turn away, Jessie realized her nose was running. *What kind of weather was this to be getting sick?* she wondered as she watched Chi roam off, looking for other photo opportunities.

"Chi, stop, you're making us look like tourists," Mike called out.

"Okay, guys," Mr. J. said. "Let's head on inside."

Kendra, who was lugging her two carry-ons, bumped into Jessie as they waited to go in through the glass doors. "I can't believe how heavy these are," she complained.

"Well, you must have overpacked," Jessie heard herself saying.

"Well, at least I don't look like I just came from sale day at the Salvation Army," Kendra retorted, eyeing Jessie sideways as she forged past her into the lobby.

Fuming, Jessie got a firmer grip on her backpack and followed on Kendra's heels. *Well, at least I don't get my face out of a makeup bag,* she almost shot back, but she noticed Mrs. Scotto, their parent chaperone, standing by the reservations desk next to her daughter, Louise. Several suitcases were clustered on the carpet beside them. One of them looked like Jessie's. Could they have found it already?

"Mrs. Scotto!" she said, flying over to the desk. The chaperone was working out the room arrangements with a clerk and didn't turn around. Jessie stood there, turning red with embarrassment as a gray-uniformed bellhop picked up the suitcases and carried them toward the elevator. There was a red ribbon on the handle of the one that had looked like hers. Clearly, it wasn't hers.

"Jessie," Mr. J. called out to her. "Come wait over here."

Reluctantly, she walked over to him and he put his arm around her shoulder consolingly. "I'm sorry about your bag," he said. "The chances are the airline will deliver it in the morning."

"Thanks," Jessie said. "I hope so." She wandered over to a sitting area. A bunch of kids were crammed onto a couch. Kendra was perched on the arm of Mike's chair. A cold sensation crept over Jessie as she found a place to sit on the carpet, her back toward them. Probably just a chill, she thought.

"Where are we going tonight?" asked Louise.

"Times Square," Justin said.

"In your dreams," Mr. J. said with a laugh.

"Hey, that's what Mike said," Justin protested.

Mike looked up from his guidebook. "Since when, O'Malley?"

Jessie really didn't care what they did. She felt too dispirited. And, though she hated to admit it, the day had exhausted her. She looked out through the doors that faced her. People passed by: in business suits, swinging heavy briefcases; in bright jogging suits; window-shopping; skateboarding. An endless human parade. A long, long way from Edina, Minnesota.

Mrs. Scotto started distributing cardkeys for the rooms. Paired with a couple of starstruck seventh-grade girls, Kendra looked less than thrilled as she flounced off toward the elevator. Soon after, Mrs. Scotto called Jessie's name along with those of Chi and Vicky, the girl who'd helped Chi with her suitcase. The three girls headed for the elevator. As the doors opened, Chi and Vicky went in ahead of Jessie. Something told her as she listened to them chat that they'd been friends for a long time. Maybe they'd just leave her alone and let her rest.

"Meet back down here at eight on the dot," Mr. J. said as the elevator doors closed on them.

"This is *so* cool!" Chi exclaimed as she opened the door to their room a few minutes later.

"This is *so* tiny!" Vicky said, teasingly poking her friend in the ribs as she went in after her.

I am so *invisible,* Jessie thought to herself. She really did feel a little left out, much as she didn't want it to matter.

"It's cute!" Vicky went on. "A little crowded, but cute." She flopped down onto the king-sized bed.

Jessie took a look around the room. It was very clean. The dark red carpeting had vacuum tracks all over it. There was a small sofa next to the large bed, and between them was a nightstand with a telephone and some brochures. Facing these was a new TV set. Flowered drapes hung in front of the windows. Nope, those budget motels had nothing on the Milburn.

She wasn't sure what to do with herself, so she decided to sit on the couch while Chi and Vicky explored every nook and cranny of the hotel room. From the bathroom came the sounds of a medicine cabinet opening and closing and faucets being run.

"Nice thick towels!" Vicky reported.

"Free hot chocolate!" Chi called out. She seemed to be in a great mood as she rummaged through the drawers in a tiny kitchenette, spotless and white, just off the sleeping area.

Jessie lay her head back on the couch and closed her eyes.

"Hey," Vicky said suddenly, emerging from the bathroom, "there's only one bed."

Jessie's eyes flew open. She looked at the two friends. Vicky was about her own height, with thick auburn hair that spilled halfway down her back. Stocky and strong, Jessie guessed that she played basketball. Her first impression of Chi from meeting her on the plane was that she was a bit sensitive and tense. Or maybe it was just that she had spent the whole flight reading a book called *Overcoming Flying Phobia.*

"Stand up for a second," Chi was saying now. As soon as Jessie was on her feet, Chi threw all the cushions off the couch and pulled out a mattress.

"Oh, cool!" Vicky said. "But that makes only two places to sleep."

"Well...two of us can share. The bed is the size of a football field."

For a moment Chi and Vicky looked at each other. Then they looked at Jessie. She had the feeling they were thinking the same thing: Give Jessie the couch.

"Listen," she told them, "I'm not feeling one hundred percent fantastic."

"Oh," Chi said sympathetically. "Then maybe—"

"The sofa bed," Jessie finished for her, coughing once.

"You were coughing on the plane, weren't you?" Chi backed away and sat on the bed.

"I hope neither of you snores," Vicky joked, getting a glass of water from the sink.

Jessie opened out the sofa bed the rest of the way, climbed in between the sheets, and closed her eyes. It felt so good to rest. Just before she drifted off, she thought of calling her Aunt Sunny, who lived in Greenwich Village, to let her know she'd arrived safe and sound. Her mother had said she should, but it made her feel idiotic. Neither Chi nor Vicky was rushing to call her family; why should she? Besides, she didn't feel she knew her mother's younger sister very well. In the past, her boisterousness had made Jessie feel very shy. She decided to wait until the morning.

"Okay," Mr. J. said when they were all gathered in the lobby shortly after eight. "Who's ready for some pastrami and egg creams?"

Jessie wrinkled her nose.

"Pastrami-and-egg *whats*?" Justin said. "This is dinner, not breakfast!"

Mr. J. laughed. "Sorry. I meant pastrami *sandwiches* and egg creams. There's a great deli only four blocks away, down on West Seventy-second."

"Let's stick together, everyone," Mrs. Scotto said. She had changed into a bright red, floral shirt. "Just follow the dancing petunias."

Broadway was bustling with people, and Jessie couldn't get over the variety—it seemed that every size, race, and age of person was represented. She tried to concentrate on maneuvering through the crowds, but found there was so much to look at that she kept bumping into kids walking ahead of her. At one point, the kid she bumped into was Mike.

"This is so incredible, isn't it, Witt?" Mike said as she came up alongside him.

"Hey," Jessie replied, keeping her eyes on where she was going, "I'll make a deal with you. Don't call me Witt, and I won't call you—"

"Okay! It's a deal," Mike said with a laugh.

She figured he would move on ahead, but he stayed close to her side, as if they walked together every day. She was very aware of his height. At one time he had been shorter than she. Once again, she felt tongue-tied. Half of her wished he would move on, half of her didn't mind that he hadn't.

"So, here's a fascinating New York fact for you," he continued. "Did you know that Broadway runs all the way from lower Manhattan into upper New York State, turning into Route 9A?"

"Really?" she said, then coughed into her hand. Her throat felt as if it was coated with sandpaper.

"Witt—I mean, Jessie," he said, "you sound crummy."

She caught his sidelong look. It wasn't mocking exactly, but it made her feel slightly uneasy. She didn't want his pity.

"It's just a little tickle," she said, swallowing back another hearty cough. "Look," she went on, to divert his attention, "that's so sad." She pointed at an old, homeless man, who was holding out a paper cup as he shuffled down the street.

Mike put some coins in the man's cup, and Jessie added a dollar. The man looked her in the eyes, mumbled thanks, and shuffled on.

"That's one thing we don't see much of in Edina," Mike said.

Jessie nodded. "My mom said that New York is one of the richest and one of the poorest places on earth. I can see what she means. Look over there..."

At the curb, a man held open the door of a limousine, while a woman dressed in a sleek, black evening gown stepped onto the curb.

They approached another corner, where Mr. J. was waiting for everyone to catch up. Jessie found herself separated from Mike. It was a bit of a relief, she had to admit.

"Guys," Mr. J. said, smiling. "Be really careful crossing the streets. Drivers and bike messengers often go right through red lights. Be sure to look twice."

"Hey, there's the Beacon Theatre," Mrs. Scotto called out just before they crossed. She pointed across the six lanes of traffic on Broadway.

A large marquee announced a long list of different music acts on various nights of the week.

"Back in the sixties, the Beacon was a very hot spot," she went on.

"Did you live here, Mrs. Scotto?" Mike asked.

"I wanted to. I tried it out for about a year, but I missed Minneapolis too much. It just doesn't snow here enough."

"Less shoveling?" Louise said. "I can get with that concept."

"So, Mr. J., did you ever live here?" said Justin.

"Nope. But I've visited enough to know that a chocolate egg cream is my favorite drink on the planet."

Justin scrunched his nose. To Jessie, it looked as if all his freckles glommed into one big mass. "Those egg creams sound kind of gross. I don't even like the kind they put in chocolate Easter eggs."

"Justin, you're a real card," Mr. J. said with a chuckle. "This is a

New York egg cream I'm talking about. Seltzer water with vanilla or chocolate syrup."

Seventy-second Street ran perpendicular to Broadway. Jessie knew from studying a map that the numbered streets ran east-west, with the numbers getting lower as you went downtown. So once the group had turned left and crossed Broadway, past a big subway station with more streams of pedestrians flooding in and out of the doors, it was on a wide, two-way avenue that was just as busy. A snack bar called "Papaya King" stood on the corner (fifty-cent hot dogs were advertised in the windows), and a little further down the street was a small clothing store, with a sign in the window that said "Nothing Over 10 Dollars." Jessie was almost tempted to go inside, but she thought of her lost luggage. She couldn't start buying new clothes now. It would be an admission of defeat, as if her suitcase were never going to show up.

"I can smell the pickles," Justin said before the group was even halfway down the block.

"Justin, stop being dilly," Jessie retorted. Several kids, including Mike, laughed at her joke. Justin grimaced. *Was he turning into Ribbet the Second?* she found herself wondering.

Sure enough, Mr. J. led everyone right into the most delicious-smelling deli Jessie had ever encountered. A big roast turkey sat on the white enamel counter, and the glass case was stocked with huge trays of pickles...*and* coleslaw, and potato salad, and countless other meats and salads. Jessie recalled her dad talking about places like this: "real New York delis." There were one or two fake New York delis in Minneapolis. None of them smelled so good inside.

The menu was about two feet high. The waiter rattled off a bunch of specials, including brisket, chicken in the pot, and potato pancakes. Each of the kids ordered something different so everyone could take bites. The table was soon loaded with sandwiches, hot dishes, coleslaw, franks and beans, matzo ball soup, and a few egg creams. Jessie slurped a cup of steaming chicken soup, which soothed the annoying tickle in her throat. She'd almost forgotten how worried she was about getting sick.

The discussion soon turned to the next day's plans.

"After breakfast," said Mrs. Scotto from the table next to Jessie's, "we'll head over to the Museum of Natural History and see the dinosaur exhibit. There might be a chance to take a peek at the paleontologists' workshop. Then, if the weather's nice, we can have a picnic in Central Park, and time permitting, we'll have a special evening outing."

"Where?" Justin wanted to know.

Mrs. Scotto smiled mysteriously. "I could tell you, but then it wouldn't be a surprise."

"When are we going to rehearse?" Kendra asked.

"In the evening, when we get back to the hotel. There's a meeting room we can use," Mr. J. said, then crunched into a pickle.

Kendra sighed deeply. "The acoustics will be *terrible.* What if we tried to book a practice room at Juilliard?"

Mr. J. laughed. "You can't wait to get there, can you, Ms. K.? First, you've got to submit your application."

For a moment, Kendra scowled; then she laughed, a big, melodic laugh that filled the whole restaurant. It sounded like a whole C-scale, Jessie thought. What a show-off.

"Anyway, get used to bad acoustics," Mr. J. went on. "We'll be singing outside on Wednesday."

"Yeah," Mike said. "Gotta take what we can get."

He flashed a smile at Kendra. Jessie noticed.

Back at the hotel, Kendra's and Justin's bags had arrived. They were waiting at the reception desk with tags on them that said "We're sorry for the inconvenience" and had fifty-dollar vouchers for their next flights. Kendra squealed as she lugged her large, heavily stickered suitcase off toward the elevator.

"Don't worry, Jessie," Mrs. Scotto said, patting her on the shoulder. "It will positively be here by morning."

Jessie slunk away. The last thing she wanted was anyone feeling sorry for her. All she wanted was her suitcase back.

Up in her room, Jessie lounged on the sofa bed. It was great to be totally still and not have to go anywhere. Chi, on the king-size bed, was channel surfing with the volume off. Iggy the Iguana, the green stuffed animal Jessie had seen nosing out of Chi's damaged suitcase at the airport, sat on her shoulder. Vicky was in the bathroom.

The chicken soup, corned beef sandwich, and extra-large

chocolate chip cookie sat heavily on her stomach. She thought about Kendra's confidence. Why couldn't she have a little of that? Not enough to make her stuck up. She'd sometimes wondered if she could be a singer, too. A professional. If you were going to sing—whether it was opera, folk, jazz, anything—New York was the place to be. She'd drawn stars in her guidebook next to all the places where singers made it big. One of them was the Apollo Theatre in Harlem, where Billie Holliday and Ella Fitzgerald started out. Others were the Bottom Line downtown, where Bonnie Raitt and Joan Baez had sung, and Irving Plaza, where Tori Amos and Alanis Morissette had played.

Her thoughts were interrupted by a flashing red light on the telephone. A message? She picked up the receiver, pressed the message button, and heard a familiar voice that, even on tape, sounded just as loud and boisterous as ever.

"Hi, Sweet Potato! This is Aunt Sunny. Welcome to New York. We can't wait to see you and show you the sights! Call just as soon as you're in. Bye."

"Who was that?" Chi asked her, as Vicky emerged from the bathroom with a towel wrapped around her wet hair.

"My aunt," Jessie said. "She lives down in Greenwich Village."

"That is so cool, isn't it, Vicky?" Chi said. "Are you going to do a lot of stuff with her?"

"Yeah, I guess," Jessie mumbled, flopping back on the bed. "I mean... *no!* Not a lot."

"You'll probably get to see stuff we won't," Vicky observed. "You'll see New York through a native's eyes." Was there a hint of envy in her voice?

While Vicky and Chi got into their nightgowns and used the bathroom, Jessie lay fully dressed on the sofa bed and let her thoughts wander. She figured she'd wait until the lights were off, then take off everything except her underpants and sleep in the buff, under the covers. *With an extra blanket, maybe I'll be warm in this air conditioning,* she thought. It wasn't something she was used to, but she figured she could manage for one night.

Then she wondered why she wasn't more excited about seeing her relatives. Maybe she would be if she knew them better. But Jessie's mother, Peg, wasn't very close to her little sister, Sunny. They were six years apart in age, for one. They also lived entirely different lives. Peg was a remedial reading teacher. Sunny was a marine animal trainer at an aquarium. Peg had never lived anywhere but Minnesota. Sunny had traveled all over Europe and lived in New York since college. Peg was careful and Sunny was impulsive. Total opposites, Jessie thought.

Vicky clicked off the light, startling Jessie out of her musings. As she listened to the other girls get into either side of the king-sized bed, she was glad to have her own. Saying goodnight, she crawled under the crisp sheets and soon fell asleep.

Sometime later, she sat straight up when she heard a sudden knock. *My suitcase!* She got up and wobbled to the door, still fully clothed, and looked out through the little peephole. A girl was shouting in the hallway. "Don't open your door!" she was saying. Then, "Idiot! You're gonna pay for this!"

Confused, Jessie opened the door. She saw the girl in her bathrobe, kicking ice cubes out of her room. Jessie couldn't remember her name. Lisa? Risa? "What happened?" she asked.

"He just dumped a bucket of ice in our room!" said the girl.

"Who?" Jessie asked.

"I don't know! I hardly got a look at him. I think he was that freckle-faced kid."

Though she was shivering, Jessie helped the girl scoop up the ice cubes and dump them into the sink in her room. Her teeth were chattering and she was coughing. At last, she got back under the covers.

Please let my suitcase be here in the morning, she prayed.

CHAPTER THREE

Stepping Out

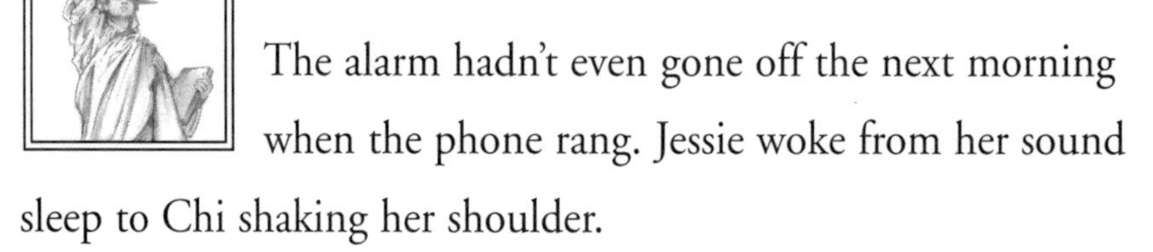

The alarm hadn't even gone off the next morning when the phone rang. Jessie woke from her sound sleep to Chi shaking her shoulder.

"Wake up!" she said. "They're bringing you your suitcase."

"What?" Jessie muttered.

A few moments later, there was a knock on the door.

"Don't forget to tip the bellhop," Chi said. "They always do that in the movies."

"How much?" Jessie said, jumping out of bed and fumbling for her wallet. She grabbed two dollars, looked through the peephole, then opened the door slowly. The same slender bellhop who'd helped Mr. J. unload their suitcases from the bus stood outside. He was holding her suitcase. "Thanks!" she said, taking it from him as she handed him the bills.

Like Kendra's and Justin's, her case had a tag on it that read "We're sorry for the inconvenience." A fifty-dollar voucher was attached, too.

She breathed out a sigh and dragged the suitcase over to her bed. But then she noticed something strange. The handle had a pink ribbon around it. She hadn't put one on hers. *Could she have gotten someone else's identical lost suitcase?*

Jessie dropped down onto the end of the sofa bed.

"What's wrong?" Chi asked. Vicky was also sitting up in bed now, rubbing her eyes.

Jessie toyed with the small gold lock on the bag's zipper. "I can hardly believe it," she said hoarsely, "but this is the wrong suitcase."

"It's what? It can't be," Chi told her.

"Mine didn't have a ribbon on it," Jessie muttered. "Or a lock." She put her head in her hands and began to cry. She couldn't help it, even if the other girls thought her a baby.

"It's okay," Chi said. "We'll loan you some clothes. Right, Vick? Mine will probably be kind of small, though…"

Keeping her head buried, Jessie listened to the conversation between the two friends as they figured out which of their clothes would fit her best. She felt humiliated. What unlucky idiot came to New York without even a change of underwear?

A couple of minutes later, she opened her eyes and saw that a small pile of clothes was sitting beside her. She thanked her roommates and tried to smile. Then, while they took showers and dressed, she called the reception desk about the suitcase mistake. They apologized and said someone would be up right away to get the suitcase. There would be another delivery of lost luggage later that afternoon, they told her. Maybe her suitcase would be with that bunch.

Finally, Jessie took a shower, and when she got out, Chi and Vicky were waiting for her to go downstairs. They must have been feeling sorry for her, she guessed.

"I'll meet you down there in a minute," she said. "I've got to make a call."

She sat back on the edge of the bed by the phone. Somehow, after everything that had happened this morning, calling Aunt Sunny didn't seem too daunting anymore.

After five rings, a boy's voice answered. "Hello?"

Jessie's throat started to tickle and she coughed into the phone. *Oh, great,* she thought. *Tongue-tied already.* "Hi, Noah. This is Cousin Jessie."

"Mom's right here, hold on," he said.

Barely three seconds later, she heard a blasting voice. "Hi, Sweet Potato."

"Hi, Aunt Sunny," Jessie answered.

"Listen, I'm racing off to the aquarium. But can we steal you for brunch tomorrow morning? Pick you up at ten and bring you downtown. We can talk about other plans then. Okay?"

"Well…sure…I guess—"

"Super!" her aunt cut in. "Meet you in the lobby at ten. Can't wait to see you, sweetie!"

"Thanks," Jessie said, but Aunt Sunny hung up almost before she got it out.

Surprisingly, her "instant hand-me-downs" didn't fit too badly, she realized as she rode downstairs in the elevator. When the doors opened, the first thing she noticed was Kendra's lime-green, silk dress that stood out from the T-shirts and cutoff shorts that most of the other kids were wearing. The second thing she noticed was that Mike stood next to Kendra. The two were having a lively conversation, as if they were the best buddies in the world. Jessie frowned. She didn't know why it bugged her so much that Mike seemed to be going out of his way to talk to Kendra.

"Jessie!" Chi called out, poking her head out of a doorway off the lobby. "Come over here."

"What is it?" Jessie swung her backpack over her shoulder and followed Chi through a conference room and into a sleek rest room, where Vicky was putting on lipstick. Chi began brushing her thick, black hair.

"Hey, those clothes look pretty good on you," she said, grinning as Jessie stepped in front of the mirror. She had on Vicky's denim shorts, an oversized T-shirt of Chi's, and, underneath, one of the brand new pairs of underpants Chi had bought just before the trip. Though she felt awkward in their clothes, it felt great to have on clean things, and she smiled back at Chi.

"Did you hear about Justin?" Chi went on, as Vicky turned toward Jessie, shaking her head disgustedly. "Well, he was going around to different girls' rooms and saying he was Mike, then throwing ice cubes inside them and running away. Mr. J. really blew his top before you came down. He said next time Justin pulled anything, he'd be out of the concert."

"I was awake when that happened." Jessie grimaced. "I thought it might have been Justin."

"How does Mr. J. know it *wasn't* Mike?" Vicky asked.

"Well," Chi said, smirking into the mirror, "Mike's kind of dorky, but he's a little more mature than that."

"I would hope so," Jessie said, blushing. *Dorky.* The word didn't fit the "new" Mike she was just getting acquainted with. But it occurred to her that she really didn't know Chi or Vicky, either. Maybe they knew something she didn't.

Just then, Mrs. Scotto poked her head inside the bathroom. "Come on, girls. We're leaving."

They hurried out.

"Okay, guys," Mr. J. said. He was standing next to the revolving doors, seeming to hold back the entire group of PYC-ers, like a goalie blocking a goal box. "Ready to rock?"

"Is the Empire State Building a hundred and two stories tall?" Justin O'Malley said.

"Is Broadway broad?" a kid named Charlie chimed in.

"Are you guys goofballs?" Mr. J. said, and everyone laughed.

"Follow the petunias!" Justin joked, though Mrs. Scotto didn't have on her flowered shirt this morning.

"First stop is H&H Bagels on Broadway," Mr. J. said. "I read that they're some of the best bagels in New York. We'll get 'em hot out of the oven, too."

New York on a sunny June morning was just about the closest thing to heaven, Jessie decided. It was perfect T-shirt weather, though the strength of the sun beating down on them promised that the day would become downright hot. And navigating Broadway proved just as difficult as it had been the night before. She tried to focus on what was in front of her so she wouldn't crash into anyone. There was far too much to look at, from all the colorful pedestrians, hurrying or strolling to their Saturday destinations, to the architectural details on the old buildings, to the chrome-fronted shops and restaurants. Not to mention all the noises—traffic careening by, ambulance and fire engine sirens, and the street conversations that she could hear only snippets of.

Mike came up alongside her. "Toto, I don't think we're in Minnesota anymore," he said.

"Hey, is it true you weren't the masked iceman last night? You aren't just trying to get Justin in trouble?"

"Witt," he said, "I mean, Jessie, why would I do that?" He sounded hurt. He *looked* hurt, Jessie realized as she glanced at him quickly.

"Sorry," she said, suddenly confused again. Somehow, she couldn't get past seeing Mike as Ribbet, goofball, troublemaker, and tease. Chi had even called him "dorky." Did Kendra see something Chi didn't? As Mike walked off, clearly miffed, she started to get angry with herself. She jogged a bit to catch up with him, but the tickle in her throat came back and she started to cough. Ahead, the group was just crossing Seventy-ninth Street. A large church stood on the corner, and another street up from that was H&H Bagels, at the corner of Eightieth. There wasn't enough room inside the small narrow shop for their group to fit, so they waited outside while Mr. J. stood at the counter and placed an order.

"Get me two cinnamon raisins!" Justin called out.

"You better hope he feeds you at all," Kendra said, "after how stupid you acted last night."

Justin shut up. He looked embarrassed, for a change. Jessie felt momentarily sympathetic toward him. Mean Kendra could really be a pain.

"I love New York," Mr. J. said with a grin, as he lugged two large shopping bags out of the store. "Instant grub everywhere. We'll find a corner of the museum steps to eat on. "

On the other side of Broadway, Eightieth became much quieter. Large three- and four-story houses lined the street.

"Some of these brownstones date back to the eighteen hundreds," Justin said cheerfully.

"Okay, Mister Tour Guide," Kendra said sarcastically, "if they're called 'brownstones,' why are some of them red, not brown?"

Just then, the group was intercepted by a pack of dogs straining on their leashes. All sizes, shapes, and descriptions of dogs, from two enormous St. Bernards down to one tiny dachshund. A muscular-looking blonde woman on in-line skates held all their leashes entwined around one hand. Her jeans pockets were stuffed with plastic bags and a wad of house keys jangled on her hip.

"Can you imagine making your living that way?" Kendra exclaimed once they passed by. "What a mess!"

"I think it's cool," Vicky said. "I mean, if you like dogs."

"Yeah, if you like picking up after them."

Mr. J. watched the small herd disappear down the sidewalk. "Those dogs are better behaved than you guys," he joked. "Okay, here we are."

"Now there's a brownstone," Mrs. Scotto exclaimed, as the group gradually stopped for the light.

Across the street was the sprawling Museum of Natural History. The massive, brownish-red buildings reminded Jessie of an old stone fortress. Facing Eighty-first Street were planetarium buildings, and beside them a park populated by people and dogs. The dog-walking skater was there, taking a break on one of the benches while her charges lay down and panted.

The "Walk" signal flashed. Everyone crossed the street and regrouped at the opposite corner.

"The dinosaur exhibit is open," Mr. J. said, "and it's supposed to be awesome."

"There's Central Park," Vicky said. "Can't we eat breakfast out there?"

Jessie looked at the expanse of green trees that started a block away. It surprised her to realize that the thick trees looked almost unnatural in the middle of this man-made city.

"It's an oasis," she said to Chi, who nodded. "It looks about fifty times larger than Lake Cornelia Park."

"Okay," Mr. J. said. "We'll take a half hour in the park now, and then go back to explore it more later."

They walked on to the corner of Central Park West and crossed over, toward the park. A paved path led through an entryway in a stone wall and to a grassy area surrounded by trees in full leaf. Mr. J. handed out bagels stuffed with cream cheese and Mrs. Scotto poured small cups of orange juice.

"Sit here, Jess," Vicky said. "Pull up a rock."

Mmmmm, Jessie thought, as Mr. J. handed her a warm "everything" bagel. It had a little bit of everything on it—poppy seeds, sesame seeds, caraway seeds, and even a swirl of pumpernickel mixed in with the dough. She bit into the gooey mess.

Kendra wandered around on the grass, frowning.

"What's wrong?" Louise asked her.

"I can't sit on this," she said. "I'll ruin my dress."

"Try that rock," Mrs. Scotto said, pointing. "It looks pretty harmless."

At last, with a sigh, Kendra perched gingerly on the large rock. Jessie watched her scrape nearly all the cream cheese off her bagel before eating it.

When almost a half hour was up, Mr. J. led everyone back across the avenue and down toward the museum's Seventy-seventh Street entrance. Just as she was going down the steps, which led through a granite archway to the glass doors, Jessie felt another tickle in her throat. It was much worse than it had been before. She started coughing so deeply that her eyes began to water.

Kendra, who was walking a few steps behind her, stopped short. "You sound awful. Where did you pick up that cold?"

Jessie whipped around so fast that she practically fell into Kendra. Fortunately, she caught herself in time. Pretending to be calm, she dug into her pack for her water bottle and took a deep swallow. "It's just a tickle," she said defensively.

"That's how it always starts," Kendra told her, backing away a step. In a loud voice she added, "Don't bring it near me."

CHAPTER FOUR

No Bones About It

Fortunately, the dinosaur halls were big enough that Jessie was able to avoid Kendra for most of the rest of the morning. And, after about a half hour wandering through the exhibits, she was convinced that she could spend her whole five days in New York just exploring this museum.

The other kids were scattered around the extensive dinosaur halls that were packed with displays showing fossilized dinosaur bones, fully reconstructed replicas, and the processes by which paleontologists find and preserve the bones. There were also interactive computer terminals to use.

She crouched in front of a display case, taking a closer look at a "Geocheline atlas"—a fossil of a Cenozoic period land turtle. Jessie felt someone crouching beside her.

"It looks like it's smiling, doesn't it?" Mike said. "Maybe another dinosaur was telling it a joke. How many T-rexes does it take to change a lightbulb?"

Jessie smiled. "I have no idea," she said, still not turning to him.

"That makes two of us."

Jessie stood up and moved on to the next display. She felt awkward with Mike. He'd teased her so much in the past. What if he suddenly turned and started doing it again?

"Hey, Jess, look," Mike said, touching her arm. "Who's that?"

She looked where he was pointing. Next to the wall, Mrs. Scotto was standing and talking to a slender man with silver-gray hair.

"I think Mrs. Scotto said she had a friend who worked here," Jessie said.

"Jessie, Mike," Mrs. Scotto called to them. "Would you round everyone up? My friend, Dr. Boniface, has a wonderful treat for us."

"Sure," Jessie told her.

"Which way should we go?" Mike asked Jessie.

"Tell you what, let's go in opposite directions."

Mike gave her a perplexed look.

"We can cover the rooms more quickly that way," she explained.

"Okey-doke," Mike said, giving her a half-hearted smile. Jessie watched him a moment. What was it with him all of a sudden?

After about ten minutes, they'd rounded everyone up and were back in the Saurischian Dinosaurs hall. Dr. Boniface introduced himself.

"I am a paleontologist, and even though I live in Phoenix, Arizona, I'm here to do some research. Mrs. Scotto and I went to high school together in Minneapolis. Luckily, I was able to arrange to take you for a quick tour through one of our workshops." Then the man's voice turned sober. "There are some ground rules. Obviously, don't touch anything. And, since scientists will be working, we'll have to go through single file. Lastly, I need to ask you to be quiet as you go through."

"Okay, guys, think you can do it?" Mr. J., who was standing next to Dr. Boniface, asked.

Everyone nodded.

"Well, let's go!" Dr. Boniface said, leading the way out toward the lobby. He used a key to open a door marked "Staff Only." Inside was a long, white corridor. Jessie found herself next to Vicky. Kendra was just ahead of them, her lime-green dress standing out exotically. *Ignore her,* Jessie told herself.

At last they came to a large, open room. It looked as if they'd stumbled into Santa's workshop, except that instead of elves making toys, there were a half dozen men and women scientists bent over large wooden worktables or seated on the floor, examining bones, creating plaster molds, and using tiny, buzzing drills to break through already created molds. At first they barely noticed their visitors, and it seemed to Jessie that the sense of concentration in the room was dense and unbreakable. But as they followed Dr. Boniface further in, one by one the scientists looked up and smiled at them. One woman even stopped her work to talk to them.

"This is a velociraptor egg," she said, gently patting the large, round chunk of plaster on the floor in front of her. "I'm using this drill to get through the plaster shell without harming the egg inside."

Justin knelt down beside her. "Why do you put plaster around it?"

"It protects the specimen from harm while it's being transported. This one came all the way from Mongolia."

"Awesome!" Justin exclaimed loudly.

"Justin, remember what Dr. Boniface said," Mr. J. whispered loudly. "Keep your trap shut."

"Are you interested in paleontology?" the woman asked Justin.

"Well, I loved *Jurassic Park* and *The Lost World*," he said, then blushed as everyone laughed.

"I loved them too," said the woman. "And they aren't a bad way to get interested in this subject. Anyway, if you'll excuse me…" she turned back to drilling.

Jessie thought this was just the kind of place her parents would enjoy seeing. She asked Dr. Boniface if she could take some pictures, and he said that was okay. A few of the kids had taken out their cameras and they began snapping away. Jessie got a picture of the scientist drilling at her velociraptor shell.

"Hey," said one of the male scientists, "did anyone see number three thousand two hundred and forty-five?"

All the workers stopped what they were doing and looked at him.

"What is it, Frank?" Dr. Boniface asked.

"A femur. It's tiny, but I had it right here a second ago." He searched the desk in front of him frantically.

"Maybe we've been too much of a distraction," Mrs. Scotto said.

"Oh, no," Dr. Boniface said. "This happens sometimes."

"Justin, what are you doing?" a girl named Claudia cried out, forgetting the quiet rule.

Justin was on his hands and knees next to Frank's table. The side of his head was pressed to the floor. His clothes were covered with plaster dust.

"Justin," Mr. J. echoed. "Get up from there right now."

"No, wait," Justin said. "I think I see it."

Frank crouched down next to him. Jessie leaned over, too, to try to see what he was looking at.

"Don't touch that," Frank warned. "It's what we're looking for." He stood up and got a pair of tweezers from his desk, and used that to pick up the femur. It was almost as skinny as a toothpick.

"Thank you...what's your name?" he asked Justin once the femur was safely replaced on its cotton batting.

"Justin O'Malley," Justin said.

Frank shook his hand, smiling broadly. "You've got a keen eye, Justin," he said.

Jessie couldn't get over it. He'd actually done something useful. Justin blushed, and Mr. J. and Mrs. Scotto were positively beaming.

"Thank you so much, Artie," Mrs. Scotto said, giving Dr. Boniface a kiss on the cheek. "This has meant a lot to us. When you come to Minneapolis, we'll get the families together, okay?"

"You bet, Dorothy," Dr. Boniface said, then turned to the group. "It was a pleasure to meet all of you."

They went downstairs to see two more exhibits. On the way, they walked through the hall with glassed-in dioramas that the museum is famous for.

"They're creepy, aren't they?" Chi said to Jessie. "Look at that water buffalo. Doesn't it seem to be staring right back at you?"

Jessie looked. "Yeah, sorta. Actually, the dim lighting in here gives me the creeps more than anything else." She coughed again, twice. Luckily Kendra was all the way at the other end of the hall, out of earshot. "That was a very dusty workshop." She hated to admit it, but she was starting to feel exhausted—and they'd only been in the museum for about an hour and a half.

After they went through the Hall of Gems and Minerals, with its sparkling displays of crystals and gemstones, and the Hall of Human Evolution, with its skeletons of early human life forms, Mrs. Scotto suggested they have lunch in the Diner Saurus cafeteria. After lunch they would rehearse back at the Milburn for an hour, and then they could rest for a while and go out again.

Jessie hoped she'd feel up for rehearsing after eating and sitting a bit. She got a tall orange juice and a Vegesaurus Burger with fries. Maybe her suitcase would be at the hotel when they got there, she told herself.

It wasn't, but there was a note saying her bag had been found and would arrive by evening.

The group followed Mr. J. to the far end of the lobby, where he opened the door of the conference room. He pulled up the window blinds, revealing a somber view of a brick wall.

"This is even more depressing than our chorus room at school," Kendra said, milling around as she sipped a cup of hot tea she'd carried all the way from the museum cafeteria. "And the acoustics are probably much worse."

"Just make believe it's a practice room at Juilliard," Jessie muttered to Chi, who started to laugh.

"What's so funny?" Kendra demanded, looking at Chi. Then she turned her gaze to Jessie. "Are you doing anything about that *flu* of yours?"

"Who's got the flu?" Mr. J. said, looking around. Jessie had just grabbed the last remaining chair at the conference table. "No one has the flu," she told him.

"Listen, guys," Mr. J. said. "We've only got an hour, so let's not waste any more of it. We'll stand around the table. No sitting."

"It squashes your torso," Justin said sarcastically. All the kids knew this was one of Mr. J.'s favorite sayings.

Everyone who was in chairs or perched on the windowsill stood up.

"Okay. Let's start with 'Oh, Shenandoah.'"

Jessie smiled. This American folk song was one of her favorites on the program. She stood next to the nine other altos, including Vicky. The eight sopranos, including Chi and Kendra the Star, were on one side of them, and the five tenors were on the other. The only two baritones, Mike and Tim Ogilvy, stood together at one end of the conference table. It was a little strange, facing the others in a circle rather than standing on risers.

Mr. J. had arranged the song in an unusual way that introduced the voices one at a time, starting with the sopranos.

Oh, Shenandoah, I long to hear you,
Away, you rolling river…

Immediately, Jessie was aware of Kendra's voice standing out from the others. There was no denying it, she had a beautiful voice—the sound equivalent of honey.

On the next signal, Jessie and the other altos came in.

Oh, Shenandoah, I long to hear you,
Away, I'm gone away
'cross the wide Missouri.

Then the tenors came in, then the baritones.

"Make it nice and round," Mr. J. coached, closing his eyes as he often did to listen more closely. "Use your breath. Good."

Jessie felt her breath give out around halfway through the song.

Her throat just dried up. All she could do was stop singing. Her face felt hot, and she knew she had to leave the room.

She was aware of the other kids' eyes on her as she slipped out into the lobby. But they didn't miss a note, and they sounded fine without her.

CHAPTER FIVE

A Surprising Visit

Jessie found a water fountain near the ladies' room. She filled a cup, sat down in a chair, and sipped it slowly. The dryness in her throat had turned into a raw, scratchy feeling, and coughing made it feel even worse. The water barely helped.

Leaning back in the chair, she closed her eyes and listened to the faint sounds of a French troubadour song through the door. For months, Mr. J. had been coaching them on how to enunciate the French words in the song, which told the story of a young man's yearning for a fair lady "with a gentle heart."

What was she going to do? Sound like a scratchy record? Why couldn't the tickle in her throat have simply stayed a tickle?

Mind over matter, she told herself. *I can make it through the next twenty minutes.* She drank two more cups of water and took a fourth into the meeting room as the troubadour song was ending.

"Are you okay?" Mr. J. asked her.

She forced a smile. "I'm fine," she said.

"You guys are sounding pretty good. I think a few of you are holding back, though. Remember, you're going to be singing outside. You've got to project." With a furrowed brow, he flipped through several pages in the music notebook. "Why don't we do the Handel once, then call it a day."

Kendra sighed heavily, her beads clicking as she tossed her braids over her shoulders. "Mr. J.," she said. "We are going to sound like duds on Wednesday if we don't rehearse more."

"No!" several kids protested.

"We'll rehearse again on Tuesday," Mr. J. said firmly. "I've already booked the room."

Jessie was unable to sing more than a few notes of Handel's "Hallelujah Chorus" and was glad when the rehearsal wound down. They had a little more than an hour before they would take a bus down to Rockefeller Center, go to the Harley Davidson Cafe for supper, and finally end up at a surprise destination.

"Please rest in your rooms," Mr. J. told them. "You all look a little tired."

Jessie was happy to go upstairs and get under the bed covers for a little while.

"Do you have a fever?" Chi asked her.

"No!" Jessie exclaimed.

"Well, it looks like Mike Ribert has one for *you,*" Vicky teased. "I saw him looking at you all during the rehearsal."

"That is so idiotic," she said from underneath the covers. "He was not." Suddenly her head began to spin. "On second thought, maybe I will take a couple of ibuprofens, just in case."

Chi handed her the bottle and Jessie got up to get some water. She felt slightly woozy as she walked to the bathroom. Almost the minute she lay down again, she fell asleep. Sometime later she was aware of someone shaking her shoulder, talking to her. But she couldn't reply. She just turned on her side away from the voice and pulled the covers over her ears.

When she did wake up in the darkened room forty-five minutes later, she felt disoriented. Groggily, she reached over to turn the light on, and saw Chi's note.

Jessie—

We tried to wake you, but you wouldn't get up. Sorry. We'll bring you back something to eat.

Feel better.

Chi and Vicky

Jessie crumpled the note angrily. *Obviously you didn't try hard enough,* she replied silently. On the other hand, why should she expect anything from Chi or Vicky? They weren't really her friends. Now she was missing out on Rockefeller Center. Suddenly she felt overwhelmed with self-pity. She missed her own stuff. She missed her Mom and Dad. She was on the verge of getting really sick.

Climbing out of bed, she went into the bathroom and turned the bathtub faucets on full blast. While the water was running, she realized she was starved. Lunch at the Dinersaurus seemed like hours ago.

Over near the TV, Vicky had her stuff laid out on a chest of drawers. Iggy the Iguana sat among a bunch of peanut-butter-granola bars. Vicky had offered these to her and Chi before, so she didn't think Vicky would mind if she took one now. She crunched on it while dipping her toe into the bath, and gradually worked her way down into the hot water, staying there until her fingertips started to wrinkle. When she got out, it was only six o'clock. She got a glass of water, grabbed Iggy, and slipped back under the covers.

This isn't so bad, she told herself, clicking the TV on with the remote.

Just then someone knocked on the door. Were Chi and Vicky back already? She hoped they'd remembered to bring her some dinner.

But when she asked who it was, she was surprised—not very pleasantly—to hear Kendra answer. She hesitated. Why should she open the door, after all the mean things Kendra had said to her? Why hadn't she gone out?

"Come on, Jessie. Open up. I'm freezing. Please."

Almost despite herself, Jessie opened the door. There stood Kendra, bundled in a purple terrycloth bathrobe. Beads of sweat lined her brow, and her pretty gray eyes, flecked with green, looked moist.

"Let me come in?"

Holding tightly to the doorknob, Jessie held her ground. But then she moved aside and let Kendra come in, hardly believing what was happening. Kendra squeezed past her. Dropping into the armchair by the curtained window, she closed her eyes with a sigh.

Jessie locked the door. She didn't sit down, just leaned on the console where the TV sat.

"You're sick, aren't you?" she said. "You were making such a big deal out of me coughing, and you're actually sick." Her body trembled with something between anger and laughter.

"Mind over matter," Kendra replied without opening her eyes. "I have to get pretty darn ill before I can't sing."

Just leave, Jessie thought. She didn't quite have the guts to say it. A commercial came on the TV. A smiling model with shining, perfect skin was applying some complexion cream to her skin. *Yeah, right.*

"At least I get a break from those girls, my roommates. All they want to do is try my makeup and hear about my trips. Granted, I've been to some pretty exotic places, but all that talking really wore me out."

"So stop talking," Jessie muttered as she changed channels to a Western movie and turned up the volume. Cowboys galloped across the screen, herding cattle. She pretended to be interested.

"Hey, can you turn that down?" Kendra looked at her. Jessie

turned the volume up another notch. The hoofbeats seemed to be pounding through her head, but she didn't care.

"Hey!" Kendra shouted. "I have some herbal stuff that's really good. Echinacea. Goldenseal. Maybe you should take some."

Jessie heard the clinking of glass on the table. She turned to look at the small brown bottles that Kendra was setting out, and must have been carrying in her robe pockets. Jessie felt curious despite herself. "What do they do?"

Smiling, Kendra pulled her long, slim self up out of the chair. "Boost your immune system, of course," she said. "Keep you from getting sicker. Got a glass?"

Before Jessie knew it, Kendra had put drops of each remedy into her glass, and refilled it with water. She'd also made herself one.

"Cheers," Kendra said, raising her glass and downing the mixture all at once. Her whole face puckered up. Jessie laughed. "It tastes awful...but it works like a charm."

Jessie held the glass up to her lips. The brownish liquid did smell kind of gross. She was only able to drink half of the glass before she came up sputtering. Now it was Kendra's turn to laugh. "Girl," she said, "I wish I had a camera."

"Ugh," Jessie said, wiping her mouth. "This is going to help?" She flopped back onto her pillow and coughed, making it sound worse than she felt. "I think I need to rest now, Kendra."

But Kendra didn't take the hint. She kept sitting limply in the chair. Jessie sighed.

"So," Kendra said after a few moments had passed, "what is your goal in life? I mean, what do you really, really want?"

"What?" Jessie was startled by this sudden turn in the conversation. "Why do you want to know?"

Kendra didn't reply. Jessie heard the clatter of bottles as they were dropped back inside Kendra's pockets. "Singing is very, very difficult, you know. Competitive. Only the strong survive. You can't let a little cold get in your way. Or your attitude."

"What about attitude, Kendra?" Propping herself on her elbows, she looked squarely at the Queen of Attitude.

"My point is, you can't let anything or anyone intimidate you. If you do, you lose."

Jessie could barely stand to admit it, but Kendra was getting to her. How did she know that Jessie had had thoughts about wanting to be a singer? It wasn't something she'd ever talked about, so Kendra's comments must be purely coincidental. Yet Jessie felt disturbed, as if the girl had seen inside her.

"Kendra, I really gotta rest," Jessie blurted out. "And it sounds like you should, too. You know, back in your room."

"Right," Kendra said, pulling herself out of the chair with surprising energy. "I can see you aren't ready to hear what I got to say, anyhow."

"That's right. Try your speech on one of your roommates later." The words sounded harsh on Jessie's lips. She could hardly believe she'd been so bold. Kendra walked out of the room without saying good-bye. Jessie got up and locked the door, and then went to pour the rest of the herb concoction down the drain.

For some reason she couldn't explain, she grabbed Iggy before getting back under the covers. It had been a long time since she felt like cuddling with a stuffed animal. Somehow, it was very comforting.

I'm better, she told herself when she opened her eyes twelve hours later. Immediately she realized she wasn't. There was a painful scratchiness in her throat that hadn't been there yesterday.

Chi and Vicky were two motionless lumps in the bed beside hers. The drawn curtains made the room as dark as midnight.

She buried herself a little deeper, her toes hitting a soft lump at the foot of the bed. Iggy. He was wedged there. She tried unsuccessfully to fish him out with her feet.

"We brought you back some dinner," she heard a voice say groggily, "but we couldn't wake you up again. It's in the fridge...probably kind of soggy, though."

"Thanks, Chi," Jessie mumbled. It hurt to talk. She still felt a little hurt, too, about being left behind in the first place.

Chi propped herself up on her elbow. "Rockefeller Center was cool," she said, "even without a gigantic Christmas tree. People were roller-skating instead of ice-skating in the rink. We went by Radio City Music Hall, too. It's very neat—all those buildings are Art Deco, built in the thirties. I've never seen so much brass detail in my life!"

"Tell her about the Human Pretzel," Vicky mumbled from the far side of the bed. She was still deep under the covers.

"Oh, yeah," said Chi, talking normally now that they'd woken Vicky up. "You know those gigantic New York pretzels? Well, right next to one of the vendors was this *incredibly* skinny guy bending his body into pretzel shapes on the sidewalk. We all put some money in his hat."

"It was pretty weird," Vicky said. "I didn't have much of an appetite after that."

"Somehow, she still managed to put away a burger deluxe with fries," Chi teased.

"Ha, ha."

"What about the surprise?" Jessie asked.

"Oh, that," Chi said. "Well actually, we went to the Empire State Building," she admitted, sounding a little sheepish.

"Oh." A surge of jealousy flowed through Jessie. Now she wouldn't get to see one of the world's greatest attractions—all because of a stupid cough! She nudged Iggy deeper into the space at the foot of the bed. She'd dig him out later—when Chi and Vicky couldn't see.

"So, what'll you do today?" Chi asked awkwardly. She sat up and swung her legs over the side of the bed. "Are you going to take it easy?"

"No," said Jessie. "I'm going to my aunt's." Each word strained her already aching throat. As if to prove her point, she sat bolt upright. It made her dizzy.

"That sounds like fun," Chi said as she went to the windows and opened the heavy, flowered curtains partway so that light blasted into the small room. "I wish I had some relatives in New York."

Vicky groaned and huddled deeper under the covers. "You better get up, too," Chi said, poking her hunched shoulder. "It's eight thirty."

After Chi disappeared into the bathroom, Jessie stood up and stretched, watching Vicky to make sure she was *fully* buried, then dug Iggy out from her own bed.

The rest of the group was meeting downstairs at nine to go over to Central Park. They couldn't have ordered a more beautiful day. Peeking through the curtains beside the console, Jessie looked down at Seventy-sixth Street, and despite her aches she felt a subtle current of excitement through her body. A line of that old Frank Sinatra song played in her head: *I want to be a part of it, New York, New York!*

When Chi came out of the shower, her body and hair wrapped in the hotel's enormous, fluffy white towels, Jessie took her turn. She steamed up the bathroom as much as she could stand it. Her mom always said that steam was good for a cold, and it did seem to soothe some of her aches and pains.

She hadn't been in the shower more than a few minutes when she heard a knock, then Chi's voice.

"Jessie, your suitcase came!" she was shouting.

"What?" Jessie shouted back. It used up the rest of her voice power. But as she quickly finished washing up, and as she wrapped herself in the last of the big, fluffy towels, she couldn't help smiling. Something was going right at last!

CHAPTER SIX

Speechless in New York

"Are you sure you don't want Mrs. Scotto to stay with you?" Mr. J. asked Jessie when she arrived in the lobby. Her twenty-four fellow PYC-ers were obviously champing at the bit to go outside. Some of them came over and asked how she was feeling. Kendra didn't even glance at her. She wore a silk scarf wrapped loosely around her neck, which Jessie assumed was to protect her throat, but otherwise she'd dressed more like the rest of them today, in a pair of red shorts and a black T-shirt.

Jessie herself was more than delighted to have on her very own denim shorts, a pretty, sky-blue T-shirt her mother had bought her for the trip, and her comfortable, worn-in sneakers.

"I'll be fine. I'll just sit here and read," Jessie assured him, and glanced at her watch. "My aunt will be here soon."

Out of the corner of her eye, she saw Mike making his way toward her. Feeling a blush creep to her cheeks, she turned aside. But she couldn't ignore his large, gangly form perched on the arm of her chair. "I could hang with you while you're waiting."

"Why?" Jessie asked, still looking away. It bugged her that no

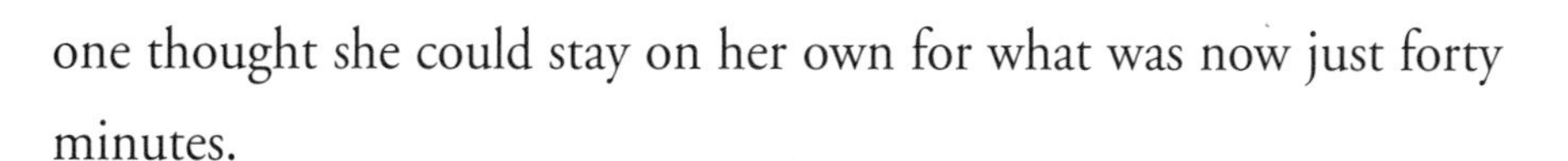

one thought she could stay on her own for what was now just forty minutes.

"My scintillating company, of course," Mike answered, his mouth widening into an old Ribbet-like grin, his eyes sparkling.

"How could I forget?"

He saluted her. "Take care of your voice. Don't talk too much," he said. "Later, Alligator."

"Bye." Jessie waved as he turned and went through the door. She felt a brief pang of loneliness. Not for *him,* she told herself.

Then she was just happy to sit quietly for a while, without having to talk.

She got a cup of water from the fountain and sipped it as she watched passersby on the street outside. Occasionally, people came through the hotel lobby, too. Most of them, like her group, were loaded down with backpacks or tote bags, cameras, guidebooks, and binoculars. You could sure spot a tourist a mile off, she thought.

Then again, she decided, it was pretty easy to spot a real New Yorker. On Friday she'd seen them carrying cups of take-out coffee, or clutching briefcases; sometimes they talked into cell phones while they walked, probably making big business deals as they waited to cross the street. She could just see Kendra with one of those phones. It would be color coordinated with her handbag. Jessie smiled at the thought.

It was a quarter to ten when she saw a beat-up red Volkswagen pull up in front of the hotel. A petite woman in an orange T-shirt and jeans, her lush black hair streaked with silver, jumped out of the passenger side and bounced—that was the only way to describe her peppy stride—through the doors.

"Sweet Potato! I am *so* happy to see you!" Aunt Sunny pinned Jessie's arms to her sides in a hug. The top of Sunny's head came just a little higher than Jessie's chin, and her hair smelled a bit like cinnamon.

Jessie felt mortified. She was sure everyone in the lobby was staring at them and laughing to themselves.

"You look *wonderful,*" her aunt went on, taking a step backward and holding Jessie at arm's length to get a better look. "I can't *believe* it's been two whole *years* since I've seen you. Why my sister hasn't brought you out here yet is another bone I have to pick with her."

Jessie laughed. She'd almost forgotten about Aunt Sunny's sense of humor.

"Okay. Save your voice for the car. We want to hear all about what you've been up to and how your trip's going. Dan and Noah can't wait to see you."

Jessie quickly stuffed her guidebook into her backpack and let herself be whisked out onto the sidewalk. The next thing she knew she was squeezed into the back seat of the thankfully air-conditioned Volkswagen, next to her cousin, Noah.

"Welcome to New York!" her Uncle Dan greeted her, swiveling in the driver's seat to give her a kiss. He had a heavy accent—"from da Bronx" as her mom put it.

"Thanks," Jessie said quietly. She felt as if her voice might go at any moment. Turning to look at her cousin, who was pressed up against the opposite door like a frightened squirrel, she decided not to try to make conversation just yet.

Jessie remembered Cousin Noah as a rambunctious squirt, when he and his parents had come out to Minneapolis two years earlier. Now he seemed utterly shy. And he'd obviously grown very tall. His curly brown hair looked similar to her own.

"Buckle up, please, Jessie," Aunt Sunny said. "Have you had any breakfast?"

Jessie shook her head. As if by the power of suggestion, her stomach started to rumble.

"Can you wait an hour to eat? If so, we'll have a classic New York brunch whipped up for you."

"Sure," Jessie said.

"To Balducci's, James," Aunt Sunny teasingly said to her husband, leaning over to give him a peck on the cheek.

"Right away, my lady." Uncle Dan faked a British accent, which to Jessie still sounded like "da Bronx."

"What's Balducci's?" Jessie asked as they pulled away from the curb. At the corner of Broadway, Uncle Dan made a right, accelerating to join the flow of fast-moving traffic.

"It's a very fancy grocery store in our neighborhood," Uncle Dan explained. "They carry fruits and vegetables that I've only seen on TV nature programs."

"Dan, that's ridiculous. They do not." Aunt Sunny laughed. "You'll love it, Jessie," she added.

Noah sighed. "It's just a *supermarket,*" he muttered.

"No, it's a *grocery*... like in the old days," his mother responded. "That's what makes it so nice, not like those big, impersonal stores."

"Yeah, Mom. Whatever," Noah muttered.

Jessie looked at him again, but his eyes were still fixed on the scene outside his window. She turned to her own and took in the sights.

Just as it had done on the bus trip into Manhattan two days earlier, the street scene flooded her senses. As weary as she felt, the energy of the city outside reached her. The endless stream of shops and restaurants, and what seemed like one caffeine outpost per block, were only a little less busy than they'd been the night before. She saw people dressed up for church, others eating in outdoor cafés, joggers with their Walkmen on—it made her feel dizzy to try to take in all the faces.

As they progressed south on Broadway, Jessie noticed a large complex of buildings a block away on the right. "Is that—" she began.

"Lincoln Center," Uncle Dan said.

"That's where we're singing." Jessie's voice came out like a squeak. She glimpsed the plaza, with its elegant fountain, and the tall, majestic windows of the Metropolitan Opera House.

Aunt Sunny turned around to take a good, long look at her. "Are you feeling okay?" she asked.

Jessie swallowed past the sore lump in her throat. It felt like extra-coarse sandpaper now. "I have . . . a little sore . . ."

"That's okay. Don't talk. I have some frozen chicken soup I can heat up, and you'll be all better."

Smiling, Jessie realized that this was one thing her mother and Aunt Sunny seemed to have in common—a firm belief in chicken soup.

They stayed on Broadway for a good half hour. Aunt Sunny and Uncle Dan pointed out the sights along the way. Soon after Lincoln Center they went past the southern tip of Central Park and headed into an area filled with huge office buildings, all strangely quiet on this Sunday morning when no one was working. She saw the Ed Sullivan Theater, with its marquee advertising *The Late Show with David Letterman.* Then there were some of the famous Broadway shows she'd heard about—*Miss Saigon, Beauty and the Beast.* There were even more theaters on the side streets. Ahead, she could see the massive, electrified advertising signs, video displays, and billboards of Times Square. It was like driving into a postcard scene brought to noisy, crowded, oversized life.

Noah tapped on her shoulder, pointing to the windshield. She saw a gigantic building straight ahead of them with a giant video display broadcasting a fashion show. "Hey," he said, "there's One Times Square—the building that they drop the ball from on New Year's Eve."

"Neat," Jessie squeaked, craning her neck to look up at it as they drove past. She'd already decided that Times Square was not her favorite part of the city. It was way too manic. As they drove through the less-bustling part of Broadway, down in the Thirties and Twenties, she felt relieved. These streets seemed more human-scale, more neighborhood-y. At one point Uncle Dan turned off Broadway and continued downtown on Fifth Avenue.

"Welcome to Greenwich Village," Uncle Dan said as they crossed Fourteenth Street. "We'll show you Washington Square Park, then double back and park on our street."

Fifth Avenue ended abruptly at the Triumphal Arch in Washington Square Park, where they waited at a red light. Aunt Sunny and Uncle Dan began to reminisce about their days as college students and sweethearts at New York University, whose buildings stood around the tree-filled park.

Jessie's thoughts turned to Kendra and Mike. She had a strange, uncomfortable feeling about the two of them. But she shook it off, and reminded herself to ask Aunt Sunny what it was like going to school in New York after growing up in Minneapolis.

They turned back uptown on Sixth Avenue to West Twelfth Street, which was lined with old brownstone buildings and some apartment houses. Uncle Dan quickly found a parking space.

"Somebody up there must like us," he said.

As soon as they got out of the car, Aunt Sunny went into action again. "Okay, Jessie, are you up for shopping with me? We'll let the menfolks put up the coffee and set the table."

"Bossy, bossy," Uncle Dan mumbled, feigning annoyance, but then he gave his wife an affectionate kiss on the cheek. Noah shook his head and shrugged, as if his parents' banter was a burden he had to bear.

Once again, he surprised Jessie by speaking to her. "Want me to take your backpack upstairs?"

"Thanks," she said, handing it to him.

Then Aunt Sunny hooked her arm through Jessie's, and they set off down Sixth Avenue. The sun was hot, but fortunately (and unusually, according to Aunt Sunny) the humidity was low, and Jessie felt exhilarated to be out on the street again. She didn't even care that the ache in her throat ruled out talking much—not that she could have gotten a word in edgewise.

"There's so much going on this week, Jessie. You couldn't have come at a better time. Did you know that I'm part of the Beluga Whale Project at the aquarium? On Friday, I'm going to be flying with a team of whale experts out to San Diego with our young beluga, Mister. Noah's coming, too. He's been adopted by Sea World—Mister, that is! We've *got* to get you out to the aquarium so I can show you around. Maybe on Tuesday?"

Slow down! Jessie thought. "Maybe," she scratched out. "Depends on what the group—"

Aunt Sunny squeezed her arm and gave her a worried look. "That throat of yours! Chicken soup and my special remedy. Actually, it was your grandmother's. Does your mom ever make it for you? Lemon and honey in hot water?"

Jessie shook her head.

"We'll get you feeling better," she said as they stopped at a food market in the middle of the block. The sign outside said "Balducci's." "Here we are! After you, sweetie."

In another moment, Jessie found herself inside a paradise of gourmet foods. Unblemished fruits and vegetables practically spilled out of bins. Long French baguettes, Italian focaccias and other fancy breads were stacked up at a bakery counter to the left. To the right and slightly behind her, a candy counter was filled with amazing-looking sweets. Aunt Sunny grabbed a shopping basket and led her around. She urged Jessie to pick out some treats to bring back to the group. Jessie stood at the candy counter for about five minutes, staring, while the patient saleslady told her what was inside the various truffles—round, button-shaped, filled chocolates made by hand. She asked for a box of twenty-five, and wondered why the woman gave her such a funny look—then she saw that they were eighteen dollars a pound!

"Sorry! Anything...cheaper?" she said, blushing (as much because she sounded like a frog as because she hadn't seen the price).

"Sure. Try these turtles," said the woman.

Jessie nodded, and got a box filled with the almond-chocolate-caramel candies for ten-fifty.

She joined Aunt Sunny, who whisked her around the store to buy bagels, cream cheese, grapefruits, oranges, lemons, pastries, and muffins. As they were being checked out, Aunt Sunny insisted on buying the chocolates for her.

"It was my idea, wasn't it?" she said. "Save your money to get something nice for yourself."

Jessie grinned. That was just the kind of thing her mom would say. "Thanks," she told her aunt.

The coffee was made and the table was all set in Aunt Sunny's comfortably air-conditioned, third-story apartment in a brownstone on West Twelfth Street. Uncle Dan and Noah were playing a game of gin rummy in the small living room, which was cluttered with handcrafted objects from all over the world. Aunt Sunny told Jessie to sit on the couch and relax—she was going to make her a hot lemon drink, then "fix her famous Eggs Scrambalaya and pop the bagels in the oven."

"Did you like Balducci's?" Noah said, looking up from his hand.

"Yeah. We—" Jessie coughed. "We bought—" Cough, cough.

Her uncle and cousin both looked at her.

"Here. Sip this," Aunt Sunny said, coming in from the kitchen with a steaming mug of what smelled to Jessie like hot lemonade. She took a small swallow, which was soothing.

"So, Jessie, what do you think of our apartment?" Uncle Dan said. As thin and wiry as his wife was, he was chubby and teddy-bearlike, down to his long, fuzzy beard. "Kind of a pack rat's paradise, isn't it?"

"Don't make her talk." Aunt Sunny fanned a spatula as if to get him to simmer down. "You can tell her about our collection, if you want." She disappeared into the kitchen again.

The handcraft collection consisted mainly of animals. Uncle Dan gave Jessie an armchair tour. There were soapstone polar bears from Alaska, a dolphin batik wall hanging from Indonesia, a painting of flying geese that one of Aunt Sunny's friends had made. The largest thing in the room was a four-foot-long model of a blue whale that, he told her, had once been in a small museum in Maine. It was very cool clutter, Jessie thought. Her own living room at home had a painting and a couple of vases in it. Minimalist was more her parents' speed.

After about ten minutes, Aunt Sunny called them into the kitchen for breakfast. They sat crowded around a round pine table, eating bagels with cream cheese and lox, the Scrambalaya—essentially a scrambled vegetable omelet—coffee, and orange juice. Noah became more animated as they ate. Aunt Sunny insisted that Jessie drink a cup of chicken broth.

"It's what your grandma used to call 'Vitamin C'—the 'C' for chicken, of course."

Noah laughed.

He and his mother talked about the Beluga Whale Project, which he was writing reports about. Jessie learned how Aunt Sunny had gone from volunteering at the aquarium to becoming a sea mammal trainer and keeper after several years. And Uncle Dan talked a little bit about his work as a theater set designer. Jessie took in every word. She had had no idea her relatives were such interesting and lively people.

"So," Jessie said when her voice was reviving, "have you always liked living here?"

"Oh, you bet," Aunt Sunny said. "I would never give it up." She gazed thoughtfully out the kitchen window. A bird feeder was hooked onto the fire escape. "How about you, Jessie? Could you see yourself living in New York?"

"Oh, yes." Jessie startled herself at how sure she sounded. "I want to go to college here."

Aunt Sunny clapped her hands in front of her face. "Your mother is going to hate me for encouraging you," she said, "but I think you'd love it here. Don't you, Dan?"

Noah rolled his eyes, making Jessie laugh.

"Jessie," Uncle Dan said, "there is one thing you need to know about your aunt. When she thinks an idea is a good one, she hangs on to it like a terrier on a bone."

"Oh, Danny," Aunt Sunny exclaimed. "If Jessie ever wants to get here, she's going to have a fight on her hands. You know how Peg feels about New York."

Jessie nodded. Her mother always said she had a "hate-hate" relationship with this town. It was why they never visited. But that was beginning to seem unfair to her: just because her mother didn't like the city was no reason for *her* not to like it...or not to want to live here.

The afternoon went by too quickly, and at three-thirty Uncle Dan said they should leave so that Jessie could be back at the hotel by four.

"So, the aquarium on Tuesday?" Aunt Sunny asked as Jessie stood just inside the front door, ready to go. "And the beach, if we have time?"

"Sure," Jessie replied.

A little later, as Uncle Dan was driving her uptown, she realized the mistake she'd made. Wednesday was the day they were performing in the festival. Tuesday, they'd be rehearsing.

And, she thought, *I may not have a voice to sing with.*

CHAPTER SEVEN

Big Chinatown and Little Italy

On the way back uptown, Uncle Dan stopped at a pharmacy where Jessie bought some cough medicine, throat lozenges, and ibuprofen. It was five when Uncle Dan finally dropped her off at the hotel. He came inside the lobby with her.

"Miss?" said an older, silver-haired man at the reservations desk whom Jessie hadn't seen before. "Are you Jessie Witt?"

Jessie nodded.

"Your teacher called. He said they were running a little late, and could you take a cab down to Chinatown? Here, he left an address."

Uncle Dan took the slip of paper, frowning as he examined it. "We just came all the way from downtown. He wants you to go back there by yourself? What an irresponsible—"

"Uncle Dan, it's okay," Jessie said, popping a cough drop. "Mr. J. is very responsible."

"Do you want to go?" Uncle Dan asked her. "Would you prefer to stay with us? We can take you to Chinatown, too."

"Uncle Dan..." Jessie felt her voice giving out. She pointed toward the elevator.

"You probably should rest, anyway," Uncle Dan said as they headed upstairs. She dropped off the chocolates, her pharmacy bag, and other stuff that she wouldn't need from her backpack. She took along the cough drops and a windbreaker, just in case it got cool later—which she doubted would happen.

Driving back downtown, Uncle Dan seemed calmer. Jessie dozed for a while, her head stuffy and hazy. When she woke up, they were on a narrow street, stuck in traffic. For all Jessie knew, they might have driven onto another continent. Chinese people crowded the sidewalks. Signs in Chinese characters hung on storefronts and restaurants.

"I won't be able to park down here, so I'll just drop you off when we find the restaurant…even though I have a few choice words I'd like to say to that…what's his name? Jay?"

"Mister J.," Jessie said.

"Don't worry," Uncle Dan assured her, patting her shoulder, "I'm not usually this much of an ogre. And at least he told you to take a cab and not a subway. But you can imagine what an expensive cab ride this would have been!"

As soon as he pulled up in front of the Little Szechuan Restaurant on East Broadway, she could see Mrs. Scotto, Vicky, and others in her group sitting at a table near one of the large picture windows. She thanked Uncle Dan for the ride, gave him a kiss, and jumped out of the car.

Five tables had been put end to end along one side of the large room so that all twenty-five chorale members plus the adults could sit together. There were shopping bags and backpacks looped over the backs of chairs and lying on the floor. Couples and families occupied a few other tables. Even with her congestion, Jessie could smell the delicious aroma of spicy sauces and roasted meats coming out of the kitchen.

"You made it! And we haven't even gotten our appetizers yet," Mrs. Scotto said to her, pointing to an empty chair.

"Hey, Jessie!" Mr. J. called out from the far end of the table. "Any trouble finding the place?"

Jessie shook her head. She hoped she wouldn't have to talk a lot tonight. She didn't feel as if she had much of a voice left.

"So how was it with your aunt?" asked Chi, who was sitting across from her.

"Good," Jessie answered, as two waiters carried over trays filled with small bowls of rich egg drop soup with tiny wontons in it. Mmmm, she thought. The soup was delicious and warming. Everyone got down to the business of slurping.

Out of the corner of her eye, she saw Kendra, the scarf still wrapped around her neck, sitting at Mr. J.'s end of the table. Her eyes were rimmed with red. For a second, Jessie almost felt glad—but she immediately felt guilty. Just because Kendra had been treating her badly wasn't a reason to wish for her to be ill.

"Central Park was fantastic," Chi said. "We rented rowboats and went around the lake, then we heard a free concert of Mozart."

"After lunch, about half of us went over to the Museum of Modern Art," Vicky added.

"The barbarians stayed in the park," Mike teased. "They wouldn't know a Picasso if their Frisbee hit one."

"Your face looks like a Picasso," Justin shot back.

"Thanks, peanut. I take that as a compliment," Mike retorted, throwing a crispy soup noodle at Justin.

Justin threw it back.

"Boys," Mrs. Scotto said testily. "Stop it right now."

Yup, Jessie thought, looking at Mike, *he's definitely regressing.*

An array of appetizers arrived—bamboo baskets containing steamed shrimp dumplings, cold noodles with sesame sauce, and spring rolls, their crispy coating filled with chopped-up vegetables.

"We're chaperoning a bunch of vacuum cleaners," Mr. J. called out to Mrs. Scotto, shaking his head as he watched everyone pigging out on the delicious food. Jessie filled her plate to overflowing, even though she wasn't very hungry after the brunch she had eaten.

"We don't need any more dishes," Kendra said. "I'm totally stuffed."

"You sound stuffed," Mr. J. commented, glancing at Kendra with concern. "I hope that this cold isn't spreading through my chorus."

Jessie put down her chopsticks. She was having trouble with them, anyway.

"Mr. J., that's negative thinking," Vicky said. "Everyone here is going to be fine for the festival."

"Well, *one* of us might not," Justin remarked.

"Oh, shush," Kendra told him. "Maybe Jessie doesn't care if she can sing or not. She's got family here to do stuff with."

Jessie picked up her chopsticks again and swirled soy sauce around the empty side of her plate. Then she looked up and opened her mouth. "You know what, Kendra?" she said, her voice cracking, "some of us besides you *do* care about singing. Amazing, isn't it?"

The waiters cleared away the appetizers. The table was silent. Kendra got up and flounced off toward the bathroom, coughing her head off.

What a relief, Jessie thought.

The table was laden down again, this time with five entrées: hot spiced shrimp with a sticky looking, Day-Glo orange sauce; beef with broccoli; lo mein noodles with roast pork; and moo shu chicken, a kind of finely chopped, spicy stir-fried hash that came with thin, flour pancakes. Mr. J. demonstrated how you were supposed to wrap the stir-fry into the pancakes and spread some sweet sauce on top of it.

"Just a thin line for flavor," he said, then added, "Think you could make one of these at home?" He shook his head. "I doubt I could."

He was trying to break the silence, Jessie knew. There wasn't any point. The kids had descended on the entrées like a herd of locusts.

Jessie nibbled at some of the lo mein, but she'd lost her appetite. Kendra stayed in the rest room for a long time, and when she finally came back, the fortune cookies were being served. It surprised Jessie to realize that Kendra's eyes looked puffy now, too.

"'A harmonious future awaits you,'" Mrs. Scotto read aloud. "See, the concert is bound to be a success!"

Jessie tucked her fortune into the pocket of her jeans. It read "Expect the unexpected."

Twenty-seven stuffed Minnesotans gathered in front of the restaurant. "I want everyone to stick together," Mr. J. told them. "Mrs. Scotto will take the lead and I'll follow in back. We'll head west to Little Italy and walk off that feast, then we'll grab the subway back uptown."

It quickly became clear to Jessie that there was no way to negotiate the crowded sidewalks and still keep the group together. Soon they had thinned out into clusters of two or three. Since she hadn't used any of her extra spending money yet, Jessie figured she could afford to buy something—maybe a gift for her mom, and Aunt Sunny, too.

Every few steps there was another brightly lit shop, restaurant, or bakery. The warm night air was permeated with the smells of fish and shellfish sold from stalls. Surprising sights were everywhere: A whole, dead octopus lay on a bed of ice; sea urchins, conch, and other unusual seafood were piled in wooden crates. A vegetable stand offered dozens of different kinds of greens, which looked freshly picked. It was like another New York.

Mike came up beside her as she stood gazing through the window of a souvenir shop. The display contained everything from embroidered silk slippers, delicate teacups, and green jade figurines to plastic mesh shopping bags and flip-flops.

"So," he asked, "is it true you've come down with the bubonic plague?"

Jessie nodded. "Yeah. It must have been carried by a Minnesota rat stowed away on the plane."

"Guess it was coming here to visit all its cousins."

She laughed, glancing up at Mike. She couldn't help it. Even if he had regressed, he'd made her feel better, somehow. She noticed again that his eyes had become awfully blue since fourth grade. Did he have tinted contacts? No, she didn't remember him ever wearing glasses.

"Anyway, that's kind of a cool vase," he went on, pointing at a delicate porcelain one painted with tiny flowers. "Do you like it?"

"Yeah. It's neat."

They stood there a little while longer. Jessie fidgeted. She was aware of looking, but not really seeing what she was looking at.

"I mean, do you *like* like it?" Mike asked again.

"Why are you acting so weird?" Jessie blurted out.

"Weird? What do you mean, weird? Like a pierced nose?"

Jessie looked at him and giggled despite herself. Mike had stuck a grain of rice on the outside of his nostril.

"Ribbet, you *originated* the meaning of weird."

"Hey...what did we agree to? No Ribbet, please." Suddenly he yelled. Jessie whirled around at the same time he did to see Justin standing behind him holding up a long, wooden stick with a hand carved at the end of it.

Mike blasted him. "You idiot! I thought you were a mugger."

"Sor-ree! It's just a back scratcher," Justin muttered, slinking away.

"We'd better go," Jessie said, noticing that Mr. J. and Mrs. Scotto were waiting with most of the rest of the group at the corner.

"Okay," Mike told her. "You go ahead. I'll catch up."

Jessie saw some pretty brass wind chimes inside a shop window that she thought her mother and Aunt Sunny would like. She went into the store and picked out two of them, which the shopkeeper wrapped in crinkly brown paper. When she got back out onto the street, she looked around for Mike, but he wasn't there. She continued walking toward the rest of the group, which had gathered at the corner of Broadway and Canal. Mr. J. wore a worried expression and was looking all around, as if he wasn't sure which way to go.

"Did you see Kendra?" he asked Jessie when she caught up with them. "We've got tabs on everyone else, but I don't remember seeing her since the restaurant."

"No," Jessie said, turning to look back up the block.

Then Louise, who stood pressed against her mother, spoke up in a frightened voice. "She told Mimi and me that she took a lot of money with her."

Mr. J. slapped the heel of his hand against his forehead. "I told you guys not to carry around a lot of cash. This is a big city—you can never be too careful." He stared thoughtfully at the ground for a moment. "Okay," he said. "Everyone wait here with Mrs. Scotto. I'll take a look."

"Where is he going?" Mike said, walking toward them just as Mr. J. was walking away. He was holding a small plastic shopping bag.

"Looking for Kendra," Chi answered. She had come over to stand next to Jessie. Most of the other kids were talking and joking around, as if everything was okay. Jessie scanned the rows of stores on the other side of Broadway. Suddenly, she had a strange feeling that she knew where Kendra was.

CHAPTER EIGHT

A Break in the Clouds

Before she knew what she was doing, Jessie looked both ways and crossed Broadway.

"Hey!" Mrs. Scotto yelled after her. "Come back!"

Jessie ignored her and drew closer to the small shop that she'd spotted from the opposite side of the street. Dried herbs hung in the window. When she got to the door and peered inside, she had the impression she was looking at a botanical garden that hadn't been watered in a long time. There were dried herbs everywhere. And there was Kendra, standing at the counter, appearing to examine something that lay there. For a moment, Jessie hovered in the doorway. A big part of her wanted to turn around and leave Kendra there. But something—she wasn't sure what—propelled her inside the store, up to the counter. She was startled to see tiny leaves packed into several glass jars and the hundred-dollar bill lying beside them.

Kendra seemed just as startled to see her. Right away, her temper flared up. "Did you follow me here?" she asked in a gravelly voice, grabbing the hundred and shoving it into the shopkeeper's hand.

"Everyone is looking for you. Mr. J. is worried about you. Don't you ever think of anyone but yourself?" Hearing the words bubble out of her, Jessie couldn't believe she was saying them. Just a few days ago, she never would have dreamed of standing up to Kendra Roberts.

The woman came back with change. Two twenties. Jessie couldn't believe it. Not only did Kendra carry around hundred-dollar bills, she'd just spent sixty dollars on some very suspicious-looking leaves.

"Thank you," Kendra told the shopkeeper. She turned on her heels and swept out of the store, with Jessie following close behind her.

"Kendra, what is that?"

"What is what?" she answered.

Across the street, Mr. J. had spotted them and had started to wave. Jessie grabbed Kendra's arm. It felt so slight, almost brittle, like a bird's wing.

Kendra whipped around to face her. "It's a remedy," she said hoarsely. "A Chinese throat remedy. I don't know about you, but I'm *not* going to miss any of our rehearsals, and I'm *going* to sing in the concert on Wednesday." Then she pulled away and ran across the street, just as the "Don't Walk" sign started to flash. Jessie ran after her.

"Where were you? What were you doing?" Mr. J. sounded angry but relieved.

"Just getting some souvenirs," Kendra said matter-of-factly.

Yeah, right, Jessie thought. She felt sick from exerting herself.

Later that night, Jessie woke up coughing and shivering. She felt as if she had a fever. The air conditioning raised the hairs on her skin as she made her way to the bathroom in the dark. Shutting the bathroom door behind her, she turned on the light, which blasted into her eyes and made her head throb with pain. By the time her eyes had adjusted enough to look into the mirror, she half expected to see the bride of Frankenstein staring back at her. But aside from somewhat bloodshot eyes and even paler than usual skin, she looked more or less like herself. She took some ibuprofen, then a dose of cough medicine followed by a glass of water. Her mom always said that the only way to really shake off a bad cold was to rest. Now that she seemed to be feverish, she wondered if her cold had become the flu. Then she wondered about Kendra's herbs. Were they working? What if they'd had some bad side effects? Kendra had the kind of self-confidence Jessie wished she had more of. Did that mean she knew what she was doing?

Deciding she didn't have to figure all that out tonight, Jessie went back to bed and slept soundly for eight hours straight.

"What did you do?" Chi asked her late the next morning, as they were walking down Amsterdam Avenue toward Lincoln Center. "Your voice sounds almost back to normal."

Jessie laughed. "I don't know. It's still a tiny bit scratchy, but it doesn't really hurt to talk." She thought for a moment. "Last night I woke up with a fever. Maybe it broke after I went back to sleep."

"Maybe it was all that yummy food we had last night. Some of those dishes I've never even had before, and my parents are Chinese." She laughed. "Well, I'm glad you're feeling better. That means you'll be fine for the concert."

"Thanks," Jessie said. "I hope so."

Chi patted Jessie on the arm and hurried to catch up with Vicky.

Two young African-American women walked toward the group, linked arm in arm. They wore beautiful batik-printed sundresses in bright colors. One of them had on a wide-brimmed straw hat. They were talking and laughing as if at a joke, but they stared curiously as the large group of kids passed them. Jessie thought they must look like a big oddity.

"Where are you here from?" the woman with the hat called out.

"Minneapolis," someone behind Jessie called back.

"Oh! You are a long way from home, aren't you?"

And then Mr. J., who was bringing up the rear, told them, "We're singing in the youth chorus festival at Lincoln Center Wednesday afternoon. Bring everyone you know!"

"Nothing like a little free advertising," Mike said, walking up beside Jessie. She felt her face redden, all she needed on a day that already felt as hot as a sauna.

"I think you dropped this back there." Mike handed her a small, folded up piece of paper. Then he hurried on ahead, toward the front of the group, where Mrs. Scotto was talking to Kendra.

Jessie looked at the paper curiously, but then stuffed the folded scrap into the pocket of her shorts. She hadn't dropped anything. Probably Mike was playing a joke on her…"for old time's sake."

Up ahead, she saw Mike fall into step next to Kendra. Suddenly, Jessie's stomach felt queasy.

Mr. J. took a left on Sixty-sixth Street. She heard someone say that The Juilliard School was on the next corner. Kendra looked as if she was dancing on air. They hadn't planned to go there, as far as Jessie knew, but she had to admit she was curious to see it after hearing Kendra talk about it so much.

She was surprised to see that it was an unassuming, modern building complex made of reddish brick. Jessie had only gotten a fleeting look at it while she'd driven by yesterday with Aunt Sunny, Uncle Dan, and Noah. Now it appeared to be a poor cousin to the other buildings of Lincoln Center. But some of the finest musicians, singers, and dancers in the country were trained in this humble-looking place. Jessie made a wide circle around the bench where Mike, Kendra, Mrs. Scotto, and one of Kendra's groupie roommates had sat down. She was curious about the note, but she had to get away from the others to read it.

She went past the building and pretended to be reading one of several freestanding, vertical signs that advertised events at Juilliard. Then she slipped around the sign and unfolded Mike's note. The print was tiny and carefully written. It was a poem! Jessie quickly crumpled the paper up again and stuffed it back into her pocket.

"Pretty bad, right?" Mike said. He was standing directly in front of her. "But it's meaningful, believe me."

"Mike, you have an amazing knack for just popping up everywhere," she replied. Her heart was beating like crazy.

He grinned nervously. "Didn't mean to scare you." He ducked behind the sign so that he was also out of sight of the others.

"Listen, Ribbet," she whispered, looking around frantically to make sure they hadn't been seen by anyone but the anonymous passersby, "we've barely spent any quality time together since... like, fourth grade. You don't even *know* me."

"What don't I know?" he challenged her.

They locked eyes for a few moments. Mike's eyes were intensely blue. But not cold blue, Jessie decided. Warm, I-like-you blue. She had to look away. "For instance, that Kendra isn't the only one around here who's serious about singing."

It came out all at once, and for some strange reason, she felt relieved to say it. But she was careful not to meet Mike's gaze, knowing if she did, right now, she'd lose it. Start bawling, or something else equally mortifying.

"You want to be a professional singer?" Mike asked gently.

"Yeah. Maybe. If I can."

"I think you can, if you work at it."

"But I don't even know what kind of singer I want to be. Or if I'm good enough."

Suddenly, Mr. J. shouted, "Come on, guys! Let's check out the fountain."

Jessie looked up. Mike was smiling at her. "Want to go?" he said.

They emerged from behind the sign and followed after the rest of the group, which was making its way across the street to "the main event."

"There's only one way to find out if you're good enough," Mike told Jessie, "and you know what that is."

Jessie nodded. "Working at it."

"Anyhow, you've got one up on me," Mike told Jessie as they crossed the street. "I don't have any idea what I want to do with my life."

"So, you'll find out," Jessie said. She was surprised at how comfortable she felt walking next to Mike, especially after her big confession.

"Jess…you mind if I call you Jess?"

She shook her head and smiled.

"Now that I know one thing about you," Mike said, "do you think—"

"Come on, slowpokes," Mrs. Scotto interrupted loudly. She stood several yards ahead, in her unmistakable flowered blouse and shorts, in front of the first pillared building.

Jessie was relieved, in a way, not to hear the rest of Mike's sentence. She didn't want to have to answer any big questions. The two of them ran to catch up.

"Wow," she breathed as she gazed at the beauty of the plaza, with its splashing fountain and its magnificent buildings—Alice Tully Hall, the New York State Theater, and the Metropolitan Opera House, known as the Met. Would she really be singing *here?* What a far cry from the basement chorus room or the Edina Civic Center auditorium!

Then she remembered Mom and Dad telling her to check out the stage set paintings for *The Magic Flute,* a Mozart opera, by the painter Marc Chagall, now hanging over the grand entranceway to the Met. Lifting her gaze up to the elegant, glass-fronted building, she saw the pair of enormous canvasses swirling with sun-drenched colors. A smile broke out on her face. Those paintings seemed to express her emotion at that moment. Joy—at being in New York, at feeling better, at the knowledge that if she put her mind to it, she could one day become a really fine singer.

And then there was Mike. She was actually starting to think of him as Mike. Had he turned from Ribbet into a prince?

Jessie snapped out of her daydream when she saw Kendra sitting on the edge of the fountain, also facing the opera house. She looked lonely, lost in thought. None of the other kids were talking to her, and she wasn't talking to them. *Saving her voice?* Jessie wondered. *Or keeping herself apart?* For a moment, despite herself, Jessie felt her anger at Kendra dissolving a little bit.

CHAPTER NINE

Discovered by a Diva

After a while, Mr. J. and Mrs. Scotto had gathered the entire group in a park just south of the Met. They stood under tall, shady trees that provided some relief from the midday sun. A large, ornate band shell stood at one end of the park, with a sea of folding chairs facing it.

"We are in Damrosch Park," Mr. J. explained, "and this is the Guggenheim Band Shell, where we'll be singing in two days."

Several kids gasped.

Jessie felt a twisty, nervous sensation in her stomach. "It's huge!" she blurted out.

"There are twenty-five hundred seats here," Chi said, reading from her travel guide.

The group pulled in more tightly around Mr. J. and Mrs. Scotto and it seemed like everyone was talking at once.

"Are we going to fill it?"

"Are there microphones?"

"Can we eat?" Justin asked.

Mr. J. laughed and roughed up Justin's thick, straight hair. "I don't know if we'll fill it, though remember we're one of fifty choruses performing. Yes, there are microphones above the stage—see?" He pointed to where they hung. "We'll have lunch in a half hour. First, I think we might have an impromptu rehearsal. Here. In the park."

"Oh, great," Vicky moaned. "Everyone's gonna hear us!"

"Honey," Mrs. Scotto said, "in two days, people are going to be flocking to hear you. Does it make a difference if a few people hear you accidentally?"

"Also, it'll give us a feel for what it's like to sing outdoors. Let's go over there, by those trees. That way we'll be off the path."

Justin edged away from Mr. J.'s side, toward a hot-dog vendor's cart that stood nearby. But Mr. J.'s hand shot out in time to grab his T-shirt collar and pull him back.

"A little culture first, before lunch, Mr. O'Malley," Mr. J. intoned, without turning away from the rest of the group. "Then we'll go down to the half-price ticket booth in Times Square and see if we can get tickets for a show tonight."

In a few minutes, they'd arranged themselves in a tight semicircle on an area of packed dirt. Jessie was surprised that Kendra wasn't saying anything disparaging about Mr. J.'s choice of rehearsal spots. In fact, Kendra was being surprisingly quiet. She stood with the other sopranos, sandwiched in between Louise and Vicky. But she stared at the ground as if she wished she could melt into it. A scarf was wrapped loosely around her neck.

A few people turned their heads to look at them as they passed by, but so far, no one had actually stopped.

Mrs. Scotto sat on a bench and watched, smiling, as Mr. J. told them they'd take it from the top. Their opening song was the troubadour's love ballad from fourteenth-century France called "Une Jeune Dame Jolie et Gentille" ("A Young Lady, Pretty and Kind"). Jessie didn't know what all the lyrics meant, but Mr. J. had given them the gist of the song when they were first learning it. Something about a beautiful lady with eyes that shone like emeralds, beloved by a common soldier who didn't feel worthy of her love.

Mr. J. held his hands up in the air, ready to conduct them in the opening note. "Okay, everyone. Ready?"

Throats cleared. A nose was blown. And then suddenly, in the midst of a busy park with birds singing, the sounds of pedestrian and car traffic around them, the world seemed completely still. Mr. J. counted a beat with his hands. He looked at the chorale members, concentrating, his eyes traveling across all twenty-five of them so that he knew he had everyone's attention. Jessie could feel her palms sweating. Would she be able to sing at all? Could her voice handle it?

Then Mr. J.'s hands came down and they hit their first notes. The lively song came out hesitantly at first. Jessie sang quietly, but her voice was there. It didn't crack or tremble as long as she didn't push it.

Mr. J. then gave them his "gimme" signal, cupping his palms

and motioning toward himself, as if motioning them to come over. The signal meant, "Give me more. Pour on the juice." Everyone responded immediately. The voices grew louder, stronger, and seemed to breathe new life into the song. A contagious smile went around the group. They were all getting swept along by the joy of making beautiful sounds. All except for one person, one voice—the best voice. Kendra remained silent, eyes cast down.

Sing, Jessie thought, looking at her. *We need your voice.*

Jessie felt her voice giving out, but she did not stop singing, and finally, the song ended. Applause and whistles filled the air. A small audience had magically appeared while they were singing—a woman carrying a baby on her back, a man on in-line skates, and a very tall, stocky woman whose green eyes were similar to those of the "kind, pretty lady" in the song.

They sang through the rest of the program, all twenty minutes of it, and when they were done, the green-eyed woman walked up to Mr. J.

"Lovely, lovely," she said, shaking his hand. "It's been a while since I've heard such a good children's chorus."

"Thank you," Mr. J. answered. "We're the Prairie Youth Chorale. I'm Ted Jacobs, their director."

"Well done, Mr. Jacobs," said the woman. "I am Miranda Tillington."

Jessie saw Kendra look up, her eyes round with disbelief.

"Ms. Tillington," Mr. Jacobs said, bowing low. "I'm so sorry I didn't recognize you."

The lady brushed away his apology with one chubby hand. “Oh, don’t even mention it. Really.”

Excitedly, Mr. J. turned around and introduced her to the chorus. “Everyone, this is one of the most celebrated opera stars in the world, Miranda Tillington.”

The diva beamed. “Thank you. I appreciate that.”

Jessie couldn’t help grinning as she looked at the shrimpy man who had suddenly appeared alongside Ms. Tillington and handed her a cold bottle of iced tea. “Thank you, Arnie,” she said, with a regal tone. “And by the way, see what you can do about getting these youngsters and their chaperones in to see tonight’s performance.”

“But, Miranda, you *know* it’s sold out,” the man replied. “We just discovered that five minutes ago.”

“Yes,” the great singer said. “Well, go perform a miracle. You’re good at miracles, Arnie,” she added, watching the thin man slouch off toward the Met. “How many are you altogether?” she asked Mr. J.

“Twenty-five kids and two adults.”

“Did you hear that, Arnie?” Miranda Tillington bellowed. With a frustrated wave, Arnie indicated he had. He still didn’t turn around, however.

Jessie wondered if he was Mr. Tillington or an overworked assistant. Either way, she felt sorry for the man.

"That's incredibly nice of you," Mrs. Scotto said. "There's no need to go to such trouble…"

Turning a hundred-watt smile on her, Miranda Tillington said, "It isn't any trouble at all, I assure you. Young people should have a chance to listen to opera, to appreciate it. I am more than happy to provide that opportunity." She began to walk up the path after Arnie, waving back at them as he had, behind her head.

The moment she was gone, Justin lay on the ground, belly down, his head almost touching Mr. J.'s sandals. "Please, *please* can we go eat now?"

That snapped Mr. J. out of his starstruck stupor. "Yes. You must all be starved."

"Someone's got to wait here, though," Mrs. Scotto said, "till we know about our tickets."

"That's true," Mr. J. agreed, a smile creeping across his face. "We're lucky ducks. Who needs half-price Broadway seats when you can have a free night at the Met?"

It took a few minutes to negotiate who was starving and who could wait another half-hour to eat. When the ravenous group had left with Mr. J., Jessie found herself sitting on a bench next to Kendra, who was sipping from a container of orange juice. Jessie saw some of the other kids lining up at the hot-dog cart to buy drinks. She realized suddenly that singing, combined with the heat, had made her very thirsty, and she took a lukewarm bottle of water out of her backpack.

"I sure blew that one," Kendra whispered hoarsely. "Here Miranda Tillington just appears while we're rehearsing, and I can't sing. I've *always* been able to sing, whenever. Even with a cold."

Jessie turned to look at Kendra, who was staring out into the distance, almost as if she'd been talking to herself.

"Those Chinese herbs I got last night?" Kendra went on, her tone turning bitter. "My voice teacher back home swore by them for sore throats. Sixty damn bucks down the tube." She shook her head.

For a few minutes, they sat silently, watching the ten other kids who'd stayed behind, just drinking sodas and goofing around. Mrs. Scotto was reading a newspaper on the next bench. Jessie wished she could just goof around, too. She felt a little trapped by Kendra's monologue.

"What are you guys going to do without me, anyway? How are you going to reach those seats all the way in the back?" She pointed to the last row of chairs.

Jessie sighed. She stood up slowly, as if Kendra hadn't been talking to her after all, and started to walk over to the hot-dog vendor.

"You always do that to people?"

She turned to look at Kendra, unsure that she'd heard her correctly. It was hard getting used to Kendra sounding so faint.

"Walk away. Stop listening. You know what I'm talking about."

Jessie was so tempted just to move away. Keep going. Get a soda and walk around the park. But for some reason, she found herself taking a step back toward the bench. Meeting Kendra's angry eyes.

She was getting good and angry herself, and the next words that came out of her mouth filled her by surprise.

"You know, Kendra," she said, "for someone with a sore throat, you sure are doing a lot of talking. If you put *half* that energy into singing, just think of the possibilities."

Mrs. Scotto and several of the kids were staring at them now.

Kendra seemed dumbfounded. She wasn't used to being talked back to. Her eyes shot sparks at Jessie. Then, oddly, the corners of her mouth turned up. She smiled. Then she laughed an all-out belly laugh.

"What did I say? What?" Jessie asked, indignant, not ready to give up a smile.

Leaning over, her luxurious braids swinging, Kendra continued laughing as if Jessie had just made the funniest joke in the world. Her two seventh-grade roommates had come over to see what was wrong. Mystified, Jessie went to buy a soda. She found a bench that was far enough from the others to have a moment's peace. As she sat there, cooling off, she saw Arnie coming down the path from the Met toward them, clutching an envelope. *The tickets,* she thought. They were going to see *The Magic Flute.* Suddenly she remembered the scrap of paper in her pocket. But she couldn't deal with anything else potentially weird at the moment. She decided she'd wait to open it until she was back at the hotel.

A few hours later, behind the locked bathroom door in their hotel room, she sat on the toilet seat cover and read Mike's poem. But it wasn't a poem, exactly. It was titled "Riddle":

I have flowers.
I hug flowers.
I am mostly water.
Without talking,
I have colorful powers.
Move me and shake me,
But by all means, don't break me.

"Mike," she said, smiling as she refolded the paper, "you are *definitely* still Ribbet."

CHAPTER TEN

Take the F Train

The Magic Flute was a huge hit with everyone. Only Kendra and one other kid in the chorus had been to an opera performance before, but not even they had seen anything like the interior of the Metropolitan Opera House, with its smooth red carpet, its wide, sweeping staircases, and its wonderful chandeliers that were raised up toward the ceiling before each performance. Though their seats were scattered in different parts of the audience (Jessie's was high up in the "nosebleed section" at the back of the hall), the stage was easily visible and translations of German lyrics of Mozart's opera scrolled by on small monitors in front of all the seats. Sometimes Jessie found herself reading, but more often she watched the stage and let herself be caught up in the music without having to understand the words.

And the music was beautiful, she had to admit. At home, she usually shut her door when her parents listened to opera on the radio. But there was something about hearing the voices live and seeing the singers against a lavish stage set that made opera actually seem exciting. The love story between Prince Tamino and Princess Pamina had a happy ending, even if they kept misunderstanding each other right and left. And Miranda Tillington, as the wicked Queen of the Night, sent chills up and down Jessie's spine with her powerful mezzo-soprano voice.

She was also surprised at how people dressed for the evening. She had been expecting diamonds, furs, and evening gowns. In fact, most of the audience was casually dressed, which helped her feel like she fit in wearing a pair of black jeans and a short-sleeved top in gray raw silk, with a black cotton cardigan to stay warm in the air conditioning. The outfit made her feel very "New York," since everywhere she went she saw people wearing black. She, Chi, and Vicky had even put on black nail polish for the occasion (Vicky's idea).

During the intermission, while she was getting a drink at the water fountain, Mike came over and gave her a small paper bag.

"See if you can figure out why I'm giving this to you," he said, grinning as he turned away.

"I *thought* so," Chi said, coming up to her a few seconds later. "He really does have a crush on you. What did he give you? A ring?" She made her eyes very wide, and she moved her eyebrows up and down rapidly.

"No, he didn't get me a *ring.*" Jessie laughed nervously as she stuffed the bag under her sweater. "He's a goofball, remember? It's probably a stale bagel, or something."

"I recognize the bag. It looks like something from Chinatown." She pulled Jessie over to a corner of the lobby behind a tall potted palm, where they could be out of sight. "Come on, I won't tell anyone."

Jessie sighed. She hoped she could trust Chi. She slowly unrolled the bag and took out the small enameled vase she and Mike had looked at in the window of the Chinatown shop.

"That's so pretty," Chi said. "He doesn't have bad taste at all."

The overhead lights started to flicker, indicating that they should return to their seats. As they walked together into the hall, Jessie pondered Mike's riddle. *I have flowers. I hug flowers.* The vase was the answer to his riddle. That impressed her, somehow. He'd gone to the trouble of thinking up a clever riddle in the first place, and getting her something beautiful to go with it. Did that mean he liked her? Probably. *By all means, don't break me.* But what did *she* feel?

After the performance, Mike met up with her in the lobby near the doors while they were waiting for the whole group to gather. He asked if he could walk back to the hotel with her, and she said yes.

She noticed Kendra staring at them from the bottom of the staircase, a little wistfully, and on the walk uptown Kendra followed closely behind them, as if eavesdropping on their conversation. Jessie decided to ignore her. If Kendra had anything to say, she could just come out and say it.

"Thanks for the vase," she told Mike. "It's very pretty."

"So, did you figure it out?" he said.

"You mean, why you gave it to me? Yeah," she said with a laugh. "It answers your riddle." She took the piece of paper out of her pocket and unfolded it again. "But what does this part mean: 'Without talking, I have colorful powers'?"

Mike shook his head in feigned disbelief. "Do I really have to explain that? Jess, I'm disappointed in you."

"Ha ha ha. Okay, Rib—*Mike,*" she corrected herself, "so what does it mean?"

"Du-uh." He rolled his eyes. "It means that even when your voice goes, you still are a really cool person." A blush spread across his face.

"Okay," Jessie muttered, blushing herself. "And the same to you. I mean, even if you didn't talk so much—"

"I know. I'd be a lot easier to take. You know, having laryngitis would be like going on vacation for me. Not having to talk all the time, what a concept! I wish I could do it."

Jessie gave him a light punch in the arm. A few seconds later, Kendra caught up to them and fell into place next to Mike. Tucking the vase under her sweater, Jessie forced herself to look straight ahead. The last thing she wanted to do right now was deal with Kendra.

"Didn't you love the singing?" she asked them. "What did you think, Jessie? Wasn't Miranda Tillington incredible? I hope she comes to hear us on Wednesday, because I think my voice is back. Weren't the stage sets amazing?"

Even though most of Kendra's questions were directed at Jessie, Mike ended up answering all of them. At this point, Jessie felt she had lost patience with her, but Mike seemed to have patience in abundance for Kendra. He listened to her and gave her plenty of free rein to gab about the opera house, the singers, what people were wearing. Jessie felt a small pang or two of jealousy. After a few minutes of listening to their conversation, she walked on ahead and joined Mr. J. at the head of the group.

It certainly seemed that Kendra liked Mike. But did Mike *like* like Kendra back?

There was a phone message from Aunt Sunny waiting for her at the Milburn's front desk:

Pick you up at 8 tomorrow for the aquarium.

Call if there are any problems.

"Oh, no," Jessie sighed. She had forgotten all about her promise to Aunt Sunny. Tomorrow another rehearsal was scheduled, a dress rehearsal—and she'd miss it.

Mr. J. sounded understanding when she explained her dilemma. "We'll rehearse in the evening," he told her. "So it's fine for you to be away for the day." He smiled down at her and rubbed his beard. "Also, I don't know what it was you told Kendra, but…thanks."

"Thanks for what?" she said.

"For talking to her like a friend," Mr. J. said.

"Huh?" Jessie looked after him as he moved away. *Friend?* she repeated silently. There were a lot of words she could think of to describe Kendra Roberts, but *friend* wasn't one of them.

The next morning, Jessie slipped out of the hotel room extra early, lugging a heavy backpack with her. It seemed like she was carrying everything in it: sunblock, a towel, and a bathing suit (for the beach, in case they went there); a disposable camera; her hairbrush; and her guidebook. She figured there would be time to read up on the aquarium during the long ride out to Coney Island, all the way at the end of Brooklyn.

"We've missed you, Sweet Potato," said Aunt Sunny, rushing forward, a cup of take-out coffee in hand, to meet Jessie at the elevator in the lobby. Jessie had to admit; it felt good to be hugged and to hug her aunt back. "And I'm very sorry we have to take the subway. Your uncle needed the car today."

"Mom, you just watered the carpet," Noah said, pointing to the trail of coffee drips she'd left behind her.

"Hi," Jessie said to him. "How is your whale project going?"

"Well, today is crucial," he explained, as the three of them walked outside into the sunny morning. Already it felt as if the temperature was climbing into the eighties. "I need to collect data on the whale's growth over the past year. Mom's going to show me some charts."

They reached the corner of Broadway and turned right. Jessie remembered that the entrance to the subway was on Seventy-second Street.

"Wow," she nodded, impressed. Then something occurred to her. "Why are you working on this school project in the summer?"

Noah shook his head. "It's a special summer program in marine biology that they're giving at the aquarium." He showed Jessie the red paper folder he was carrying. It had the aquarium's logo on it. "But I can use anything I do for school reports next year."

"Big sixth grader," Aunt Sunny said with pride in her voice.

Noah, who was turning red, gave her a gentle poke in the ribs. "Mom," he groaned.

"Humor your old mother a little, okay?" she joked back.

Jessie laughed.

"Anyway," Noah went on, turning back to her, "this is a really cool week to be at the aquarium, because they're getting Mister ready for his trip to San Diego."

They approached some street vendors selling sunglasses, and Aunt Sunny stopped to buy a pair with small, round, cherry-red rims. She didn't try them on. Jessie was pretty sure they were a child's pair, though she didn't say anything about it. She stifled a laugh as Aunt Sunny put them on.

"How do you get a whale ready for a plane trip?" Jessie asked Noah.

"Sounds like there should be a punch line to that one, doesn't it?" Aunt Sunny said, giggling.

They reached the subway entrance and went inside. Masses of commuters swarmed behind them, practically pushing them through the turnstile. New Yorkers must have pretty strong herd instincts, she thought to herself. But she wondered if she'd go nuts, living with such crowds every day.

Once they were waiting on the platform, Aunt Sunny and Noah resumed telling her some of the basics of whale transport. It didn't sound like much fun for anyone—especially the whale. When he got to the other end, however, he'd have a huge tank to share with several other young whales, unlike the smallish holding tank he was in at Coney Island.

"He's a born and bred Brooklyn whale," Aunt Sunny mused as they stepped onto a downtown Number Nine train. "I was there at his birth."

"He's only three," Noah added.

They had to stand until Fifty-ninth Street, where they changed to an A train heading to Brooklyn.

"This is an express. It should go quickly," Noah reassured her.

Jessie hardly cared. She was enjoying her extended family more than she ever imagined she would. Sitting side by side, Aunt Sunny and Noah looked like two peas in a pod—and she imagined she may have looked a bit like a third pea. She told them about the past couple of days, how she'd found her voice again, and about Miranda Tillington and the tickets to *The Magic Flute.* She felt comfortable enough to give a nutshell summary of all that had happened with

Kendra, too. "You know something?" she finally told them. "We have to get together more than once every few years."

"Now go home and tell your mom and dad that," Aunt Sunny said. "Tell them New York isn't so bad, and they could come out here once in a while."

"It isn't bad at all," Jessie agreed, gauging from Aunt Sunny's tone of voice that she'd hit on a sensitive topic. Shaking her head, she added, "I don't really understand what they have against it."

Aunt Sunny laughed and reached over to pat her head. "It's too big for them. They don't like the *swirl* of New York. Know what I mean, Jess? This place is like an enormous blender. You just have to be willing to go with the flow, and then it's great."

A man with a ferret on his shoulder walked through the car, and passed them at that moment. The three of them laughed.

"If this is a blender, where's my strawberry shake?" Noah said, and they all laughed some more.

Finally they arrived in Brooklyn and changed trains for the last time, to the F, which would take them all the way out to Coney Island. There were few people on their train. Most people commuted toward Manhattan, not away from it as they were doing.

They had already been on subway trains for forty minutes, and Aunt Sunny estimated it would take them another thirty to ride through Brooklyn. Fortunately, the subway tracks soon popped up aboveground, providing a vista of rooftops, backyards, and streets laid out in that even grid system that made the city seem orderly in all its vastness. Looking out into the distance, past the crisscrossed highway overpasses and merging roadways filled with speeding trucks and cars, beyond the billboards and the laundry strung out between windows, Jessie could see New York Harbor and the Statue of Liberty. Even from this far away, the statue had a still, calm presence, which was especially reassuring in "Blender City."

Again the question ran through her mind: *Could I live here? What would it take?*

They went through a series of different neighborhoods, which Aunt Sunny named for her. Park Slope. Borough Park. Sheepshead Bay. And finally arrived at West Eighth Street Station, where there was a sign for the aquarium. There were pigeon droppings all over the platform where they exited, and they made their way quickly to an aboveground ramp, following the sign to the aquarium. In a couple of minutes they were out in the hot sun, on a crowded boardwalk next to a beach.

"The ocean!" Jessie cried out, amazed.

"Well, it's really just Jamaica Bay," Aunt Sunny explained. "But it leads to the ocean."

Jessie didn't care. She ran through the crowd and stood at the railing, looking out at the sparkling blue water. "Compared to this," she said, "the Great Lakes don't look so enormous."

"You can get a really good view of the ocean from there," Noah said, pulling her around to look at the old roller coaster smack in the middle of Coney Island Amusement Park. "The Cyclone is one of the country's oldest roller coasters."

Aunt Sunny laughed. "It's okay to say no, Jessie. I always do."

"Well," Jessie said, "I'll ride it. Why not?" She was feeling so happy to see the ocean that she temporarily forgot how scared she was of coasters.

They made their way down the boardwalk to the arched aquarium entrance. The woman in the ticket booth smiled and waved at them. Aunt Sunny said hello and then they passed through to the inside of the building. Soon, however, they passed through another doorway and went outside into the sunlight again. Aunt Sunny told Noah to take Jessie to see Mister while she dropped off her briefcase in her office.

"The trainer who feeds Mister let me pet him, once," Noah told her as they went up a flight of stairs past a California seal tank. The seals were sunning themselves on rocks while visitors took pictures of them. "Maybe he'll let you, too, once he knows you're with us."

Noah ducked under a chain blocking off a stairway, and they climbed up to an enclosed pool. "We're standing on top of the beluga tank," he said, and as he did, one shiny, round, white head, then another, bobbed up out of the water. Excited, but moving slowly, Noah opened the door that led into the pool enclosure. "The smaller one is Mister. The big one's his mother."

Following Noah's example, Jessie crouched quietly by the pool.

She still would have rather gone to the beach, and she hoped they would have time for that.

"Mister, Mister," Noah said in a low, calm voice. "It's me, Noah. Come meet my cousin."

In a matter of moments, one of the white heads surfaced again. Jessie gasped. The beluga's blue eye was looking right at her!

"Is that him?" she whispered.

Noah nodded. Mister swam, keeping his eye on them, all the way to the other end of the pool, then turned around and swam back again, looking at them with his other eye. Jessie and Noah laughed. As Mister lifted his head higher out of the water, he showed that he was smiling, too. Jessie knew that it was probably just the permanent shape of his mouth, but she couldn't help thinking he must be as happy as they were.

Then Mister came over to the edge of the pool, blowing out of his blowhole as he did. The spray hit Noah.

"Hey, are you messing with me?" he joked, wiping the water from his eye.

Mister put his head over the side of the pool. Noah bent over and kissed it. Jessie opted for giving him a gentle pat. Then they watched the whale sink back down into the pool.

Soon, Aunt Sunny joined them and they took a tour of the rest of the aquarium. They stopped at Aunt Sunny's office so Jessie could see it and Noah could get the data he needed on Mister. Before they got back on the subway to head home, Noah reminded Jessie about her promise to ride the Cyclone.

"It wasn't exactly a *promise,*" she said, but he looked so disappointed that she added, "Well, okay."

She had second thoughts as they buckled themselves into the old, battered roller-coaster car.

"You can still change your mind," Aunt Sunny called out from behind the gate.

Then Jessie felt Noah's hand grasping her arm. "You'll be okay," he said, squeezing it before he let go. "Just relax."

"Sure," she said. Her stomach lurched as they climbed the first hill. But pretty soon she was screaming and laughing along with everyone else.

CHAPTER ELEVEN

Sing a New York Song

Jessie got back to the Milburn at ten to five and found everyone else gathered in the conference room, talking and milling around. For a moment she panicked—had she come too late?—but then she saw Mr. J. distributing photocopied sheets across the room. Mike caught her eye and waved at her, smiling in a somewhat puppy-doggish kind of way. She gave him a quick smile and hoped that her slight sunburn hid the blush that spread all over her face. Then she found Chi and sat with her on the windowsill, talking about her day.

It had been wonderful—and interesting. Aunt Sunny was a cool person and had made Jessie feel completely at home in New York. Fortunately, Jessie would have one more chance to see her since she, Noah, and Uncle Dan would be coming to the concert tomorrow. Already she was thinking of how she would convince her parents to visit New York.

After coming off the Cyclone—once Jessie's stomach had returned to ground level—they'd decided to delay going home a while longer. They'd bought hot dogs, fries, and sodas at Nathan's and had a picnic on a boardwalk bench. Then, at Jessie's request, they went down to the beach and sunned and swam for about an hour.

"We took a Circle Line cruise around Manhattan this morning," Chi told her. "It was great, but I got a little seasick." Then she leaned in closer to Jessie and whispered, "Did you notice who's not here?"

Jessie looked around the room.

"Kendra?" she mouthed, even though it was obvious the girl was missing. "Where is she?"

"Some family matter," Chi whispered back.

"All right," Mr. J. said. "Let's get started now." He paced back and forth in front of the room a few times, then stopped and looked out at them with a serious expression. "Imagine that I am the first row of the audience at the band shell. You have to project your voices so I can hear it...but also so that the people ten rows in back of me can hear it." He paused and cupped his hands in front of his mouth, as if warming them. Then he looked up again. "We're also up against traffic noise, breezes, *anything* out in the environment. So use everything you've got."

Justin O'Malley raised his hand. Mr. J. rolled his eyes.

"What is it, Mr. O'Malley?"

"What if a fire truck goes by? Should we still keep singing?"

"Yes, Mr. O'Malley. Just sing louder." Mr. J. took his position, feet slightly spread and his knees a little bit bent, as if ready to spring into action.

The room grew hushed. Mr. J.'s hands went up. Everyone watched them bob several times until they came down. Jessie smiled as she heard her voice—loud and clear, without any scratchiness.

They moved through the songs listed on the program that Mr. J. had handed out. After the troubadour ballad, they sang the "Hallelujah Chorus" from Handel's *Messiah.*

It was during the middle of this second piece that Kendra slipped quietly into the room and took her place among the seven other sopranos.

Would she sing? Jessie wondered, glancing at Kendra. Everyone, she imagined, must have been wondering the same thing.

Then Kendra's voice—beautiful and clear—came pouring out into the room, adding its richness to the already lovely sounds being made. Through the rousing last notes of Handel, on through "Oh, Shenandoah" and the two pop songs on their program, "Morning Has Broken" and "Teach Your Children," and finally ending with "Amazing Grace," each of the singers gave their best.

"Bravo, bravo!" Mr. J. called out after the last notes faded in the air. "If you are this together tomorrow, guys, you will be *brilliant.*" Pausing, he looked from Kendra to Jessie. "I'm glad you girls are all better. You sound just fine."

Jessie glanced over at Kendra, who was looking back at her with a hint of a smile.

Later that night, after an evening visit to the World Trade Towers to see the view, the group came back uptown and had dinner at

Patsy's Pizza. The thin-crust pizzas, filled with all sorts of gourmet toppings like fresh mozzarella, basil, and artichokes, were scrumptious.

As they were walking back to the hotel, Kendra came up beside Jessie. "Can I talk to you?" she said.

Startled, Jessie's heart pounded hard. Was her great day about to be ruined?

"Not here," Kendra explained. "Later. At the hotel."

"Okay," Jessie mumbled. Right away she wished she hadn't agreed. What could Kendra possibly have to say to her?

She was still perplexed when Kendra knocked on her door a little later.

"Let's go down to the lobby," she said.

Great, Jessie thought. *With my luck, we'll probably get stuck between floors.*

They rode down to the empty lobby. Kendra led her over to the chairs.

"So, what is it?" Jessie said once they'd sat down. Suddenly, she felt a steely wave of anger, as if anything Kendra said would hurt.

Kendra sighed. Her chin dropped to her chest.

When she lifted her face, Jessie saw that she had no makeup on. Jessie's mouth fell open.

"I want to apologize, okay? For not being so nice. It doesn't have anything to do with you."

The words came out in a rush. Jessie was still getting used to

Kendra without heaps of eyeliner, mascara, and lipstick. Now she had to get used to her being sorry. It was almost too much.

"What would you do if everything you wanted, everything you *dreamed* about doing, were just eight blocks away? And what if you had a family that had messed up anything you ever really, truly wanted to do…and that was about to do it again?"

"Juilliard?" Jessie said, pulling her hair back into a ponytail.

Kendra nodded grimly, and sighed again. "See, today was going to be my day. I was going to meet an advisor at Juilliard, and talk to her about early admissions. But then my idiot sister, who never, ever comes home to visit *us,* said she had to see me."

"You have a sister who lives here?" Jessie asked, amazed that Kendra hadn't ever mentioned it.

Nodding, Kendra played with the beaded end of one of her cornrows. "My big sister who hates my dad. I can't blame her for that. He didn't want her coming to New York, either." Kendra paused a moment, her lips pursed, thoughtful. "If it weren't for my mom, she wouldn't have made it here—and I wouldn't have, either."

"But I thought you traveled all over the world," Jessie said.

"Uh huh," Kendra said. "Under the oh-so-watchful eye of my control-freak father. For him, life is just a guided tour you pay for. He doesn't like any of us reaching too far. The minute my sister turned eighteen, she shot out of Edina faster than a stampeding moose."

Jessie didn't know what to say. She half wanted to sympathize with Kendra and half wanted to walk away. Partly, it was just that she hadn't forgiven her.

"So I see you, a cute girl with everything you want, parents who obviously want you to succeed, some family here in New York that you want to visit, and a cool guy with a crush on you..."

Mike? Kendra thought Mike was cool?

"...anyway, I was...it bugged me."

Jessie shrugged. She sat there staring at the pattern in the rug. *Kendra jealous of me?* I don't believe it. Her mind felt like an overloaded circuit. "You have so much going for you, Kendra," she said in a quiet voice. "There's no reason for you to envy me. You've got ten times the determination I have. And as for Ribbet...I mean, Mike," she added, "I've known him since fourth grade. We're just...starting to be friends."

Kendra snorted. "Girl, getting a present from a boy is more than 'just friends.'"

"And my parents have no idea what I want to be, because...to tell the truth...I don't, either. I know I love to sing, and maybe I'll become a singer. Or maybe I'll go to veterinary school." She smiled. "It's all up in the air, and that's fine. I'm just fourteen."

With a laugh, Kendra slapped her bare knees and stood up. "Well, I'm just fifteen. It'll be a couple of years before I'm ready for a place like Juilliard."

Jessie stood up, too. "You'll get there," she said. "I have absolutely no doubt about it."

Kendra put out her hand. "Friends?" she asked. "Or let's put it this way—potential friends?"

With a laugh, Jessie shook on it. "Potential friends," she agreed.

The weather was beautiful the next afternoon, as the Prairie Youth Chorale made their way up to the band shell. The audience was packed. Jessie had no idea where all the people had come from. Some, at least, were members of the other choruses. Others, in business clothes, looked as if they were on their lunch breaks.

She felt proud of how everyone looked: the girls in long, black skirts and white tops, and the boys in black suits and white shirts. Both boys and girls wore crisp, red bow ties around their necks.

Aunt Sunny, Uncle Dan, and Noah were out there. She'd seen them on the way up to the band shell.

Looking out on that sea of faces, Jessie felt her throat tighten. *Oh, no,* she thought. Was her sore throat coming back?

But then she focused on Mr. J., his bright smile, his hands raised in the air. When they fell, a burst of marvelous sound rose up around her. In it she could hear her own voice, distinct and strong. It joined seamlessly with the other altos' voices, harmonized with the sopranos', tenors', and baritones'. Yet it was one-hundred-percent her own.

Jessie Witt, a singer in New York.

A PYC Guide to New York

Remember, opening times and phone numbers change sometimes, so you'll probably want to call ahead when you plan to visit these places.

① American Museum of Natural History

There is something for everyone in this enormous museum. Jessie went wild over the biodiversity exhibit, with a simulated rainforest that looks so real. Mike could have spent the rest of the trip (well, almost) in the dinosaur halls, and Kendra's top picks were the Hall of Gems and Hall of Minerals ("a crystal-lover's paradise"). The Imax films are always worth checking out, and the newly refurbished Hayden Planetarium reopened early in 2000. Seminars, lectures, and workshops are available to the general public on subjects such as paleontology, astronomy, and biodiversity.

Central Park West between West 77th and West 81st Streets. ☎ (212) 769-5000. Sunday–Thursday 10 a.m.–5:45 p.m., Friday, Saturday 10 a.m.–8:45 p.m. Admission charged.

② Aquarium for Wildlife Conservation

"Feeding time in the penguin tank looks like our school cafeteria at lunchtime," Jessie told Mike after her visit. "Yeah, but I'm sure the penguins have better manners," he said. From the dolphins and whales to the stingrays, sharks, and starfish, Jessie wasn't bored for a minute.

Surf Avenue between Ocean Parkway and West 10th Street, Brooklyn. ☎ (718) 265-3400. Monday–Friday 10 a.m.–5 p.m., Saturday, Sunday 10 a.m.–6 p.m. Admission charged.

③ Balducci's

"A food fiend's paradise," Aunt Sunny called this bursting-at-the-seams gourmet Italian market. Jessie had never seen so many varieties of cheeses, meat, smoked fish, candy, bread, and produce in her life. Her advice? "Bypass the canned snails and go right for the chocolate."

424 6th Avenue at West 9th Street. ☎ (212) 673-2600. Open daily, 7 a.m.–8:30 p.m.

④ Beacon Theatre

Mrs. Scotto saw a Grateful Dead concert here in the early '70s. (Mike couldn't help asking, "You listened to the Grateful Dead?") "I wore my first love beads that night," Mrs. Scotto reminisced, "though that huge, elegant old theater was really made for pearls."

2124 Broadway, between West 74th and West 75th Streets. ☎ (212) 496-7070. Admission charged.

⑤ Central Park

Chi's favorite part of the city. Why? "No stress!" Her must-sees: The Lake ("for rowboating"), the Carousel, the Great Lawn ("for people-watching and outdoor concerts"), and Belvedere Castle ("for imagining you're in Scotland"). Sometimes called "the lungs" of New York City, this proved a favorite New York venue for several PYC-ers.

It is possible to enter the park at numerous points along Central Park West, 5th Avenue, and 110th Street.

⑥ Chinatown

"The best place to eat authentic Chinese food, and a fascinating neighborhood to boot," Mr. J. called this part of lower Manhattan. Next to egg creams, Chinese dumplings were Mr. J.'s favorite New York fare. Mike found this was a great place for cool souvenirs, too. Aside from Jessie's vase, he picked up a bunch of enameled chopsticks for his older sister's creative hairstyles, and a good-luck frog charm for his little sister.

⑦ Circle Line

Justin would never forget the "nutty" tour guide who told all the passengers not to jump ship, just in case the baby alligators people used to buy as pets (and then flush down the toilet) were living in the Hudson River. Chi loved the views, especially of the World Trade Towers and other skyscrapers at the tip of Manhattan. The 3-hour cruise circles all of the island.

Pier 83, 12th Avenue north of West 42nd Street. ☎ (212) 563-3200. Admission charged. Sails every day at noon except Tuesday and Wednesday. Complimentary shuttle service is available from midtown to Pier 83.

⑧ Coney Island

Normally a landlocked Midwesterner, Jessie found walking the boardwalks along the beach a wonderful treat. "The hot dogs and fries are worth every ounce of grease," she told Aunt Sunny after a visit to Nathan's Famous. The antiquated Astroland amusement park filled with creaky rides made Jessie feel as if she were stepping back into another era.

Astroland: Surf Avenue between Ocean Parkway and West 37th Streets, Brooklyn. ☎ (718) 372-0275. Open daily noon to midnight, weather permitting.

⑨ Ed Sullivan Theater

This '20s-era Broadway theater was on Mike's list of places to see, because one of his favorite TV programs, *Late Show with David Letterman,* is taped there. He was disappointed to learn that tickets must be ordered 3 to 4 months in advance! (Send a postcard to Dave Letterman Tickets, 1697 Broadway, New York, NY 10019.) Home of the former Ed Sullivan Show from 1948 to 1971, this is also the theater where the Beatles and Elvis Presley were introduced to TV audiences.

1697 Broadway between West 53rd and West 54th Streets. ☎ (212) 975-2476.

⑩ The Empire State Building

Mr. J. surprised everyone with a 10 p.m. visit to the observation deck of this famed skyscraper (now the sixth largest in the world). The views, as he put it, "ain't bad"—up to 50 miles on a clear day or night.

350 5th Avenue at West 34th Street. ☎ (212) 736-3100, ext. 73. Admission charged. Observation decks on the 86th and 102nd floors are open daily 9:30 a.m. to midnight. The last elevator up leaves at 11:30 p.m.

⑪ Fine and Shapiro

Jessie discovered that New Yorkers, like Midwesterners, enjoy big portions. Her corned beef sandwich was stacked with four inches of meat, and the chocolate chip cookie she got for dessert was about eight inches in diameter. But she also quickly found out that it was okay—even expected—to ask for a doggie bag.

138 West 72nd Street between Columbus and Broadway. ☎ (212) 877-2874. Open daily 11 a.m.–10 p.m.

⑫ Greenwich Village

Hip, cool, hot, jumping…all those words applied to Jessie's favorite part of the city along the Hudson River in lower Manhattan. Boutiques, cozy cafés and restaurants, offbeat art galleries, and an easy-going mood are its trademarks.

⑬ Harley Davidson Cafe

The burger that Chi and Vicky brought back for Jessie didn't seem appealing after sitting in the refrigerator all night, but Jessie enjoyed hearing the girls' take on their visit to this bustling, hopelessly trendy restaurant where motorcycles are suspended from the ceiling.

1370 6th Avenue at West 56th Street. ☎ (212) 245-6000. Open daily 11:30 a.m.–11:45 p.m.

⑭ The Juilliard School

Kendra was disappointed not to have visited this prestigious performing arts school. "If we sounded half as good as a Juilliard chorus, we'd be lucky," she told Mr. J.

60 Lincoln Center Plaza. ☎ (212) 799-5000.

⑮ Lincoln Center

The PYC sang here! In a word, Jessie would describe this performing arts center as "magnificent." Whether or not you get tickets for a music or dance event (though this is highly recommended), Lincoln Center is definitely worth a visit. The central fountain is a favorite meeting place, with a rim to perch on and people watch. The chorale had a chance to take a peek inside all the main buildings. These include Avery Fisher Hall, home of the New York Philharmonic; the New York State Theater, home to the New York City Ballet and the New York City Opera; and of course the Metropolitan Opera House, with its 10-story colonnade and impressive glass walls. Other buildings include Alice Tully Hall, the Walter Reade Theater, and the New York Public Library for the Performing Arts.

Just off Broadway between West 62nd and West 66th Streets.
☎ (212) 875-5000.

⑯ Little Italy

Mrs. Scotto scoped out a great *pasticceria* (pastry shop) where the group had a sweet treat after Chinatown. Kendra, ever dieting, was the only one who didn't order anything. Jessie tried a cannoli—a crispy, rolled pastry shell filled with scrumptious crème. As far as she was concerned, dieting could wait.

⑰ The Museum of Modern Art

Chi changed her mind about not liking modern art here, especially when she saw one of her favorite paintings, Van Gogh's *Starry Night.* Mike's exhibit of choice was of George Segal's life-size, ultrarealistic sculptures of people who looked like they would walk up and shake your hand (if they weren't made of bronze). Add in the Picassos, Pollacks, O'Keeffes, and you've got one world-class art museum.

11 West 53rd Street between 5th and 6th Avenues.
☎ (212) 709-9480. Admission charged. Open every day except Wednesday. Monday, Tuesday, Thursday, Saturday, and Sunday 10:30 a.m.–6:00 p.m.; Friday 10:30 a.m.–8:30 p.m.

⑱ Radio City Music Hall

Vicky begged Mr. J. to get tickets for a Rockettes performance, but they were on tour. The chorale members did get a peek at the posh, 5,882-seat hall, bigger than anyone had seen (aside from the Minneapolis Superdome).

1250 6th Avenue at West 50th Street. ☎ (212) 247-4777. Admission charged.

⑲ Rockefeller Center

According to Chi, "the cool Art Deco details" were the highlights of this large complex of office and entertainment buildings. Mr. J. had once been to the Rainbow Room, an elegant restaurant with live bands and dancing that would take you right back to the '40s.

Bordered by 5th and 7th Avenues, West 48th and West 52nd Streets. One-hour tours of NBC Studios are available daily from 9:15 a.m. to 4:30 p.m. at 30 Rockefeller Plaza, ☎ (212) 664-4000, or take a spin on the skating rink between 49th and 50th Streets off 5th Avenue, ☎ (212) 332-7654. Admission charged for tours and skating. Open daily for ice skating from October until March, Monday–Friday, 9 a.m.–10:30 p.m.; Saturday, 8:30 a.m.–midnight; Sunday, 8:30 a.m.–10 p.m.

⑳ Statue of Liberty and Ellis Island Museum of Immigration

"This must be the world's first Stair Master," Justin said of the 300-plus steps leading up to the crown of "Lady Liberty." "But what a view," he added. Standing in the Verrazano Narrows between Brooklyn and Staten Island, the statue has been welcoming visitors and immigrants to New York since 1886. The museum is housed in the same buildings where immigrants were cleared for entry into the United States early in the 20th century. Also a must-see.

Daily ferry service from Castle Clinton in Battery Park. ☎ (212) 269-5755. Statue of Liberty and Museum of Immigration ☎ (212) 363-3200. Daily 9:30 a.m.–3:30 p.m., extended hours July and August. Admission charged.

㉑ Times Square

"Frantic," "glitzy," "awesome" were how most PYC-ers described this hub of the New York City entertainment world, though to Jessie, "overkill" was the word that sprang to mind. The hub of the Broadway theater district, Times Square is named after *The New York Times,* whose offices are on 43rd Street. It's perhaps most famous for the internationally broadcast New Year's Eve "party" held here each year. Mobs of people in the streets count down to midnight as they watch a large ball travel down a flagpole on the roof of One Times Square.

Between West 42nd and West 47th Streets at Broadway and 7th Avenue.

㉒ TKTS

This is *the* spot for half-price tickets to Broadway and Off-Broadway shows on the day of performance. "The lines are a severe test of one's patience," Mrs. Scotto commented, "but the discount is sublime."

West 47th Street and Broadway and 2 World Trade Center (mezzanine level) ☎ (212) 768-1818, both locations. Call for hours.

㉓ World Trade Center

Seated at the southern tip of Manhattan Island, at 110 stories the Twin Towers are the tallest buildings in the city. The PYC-ers went up to the 107th-floor observation deck the night before the chorus festival. "Seeing the entire island spread out below leaves

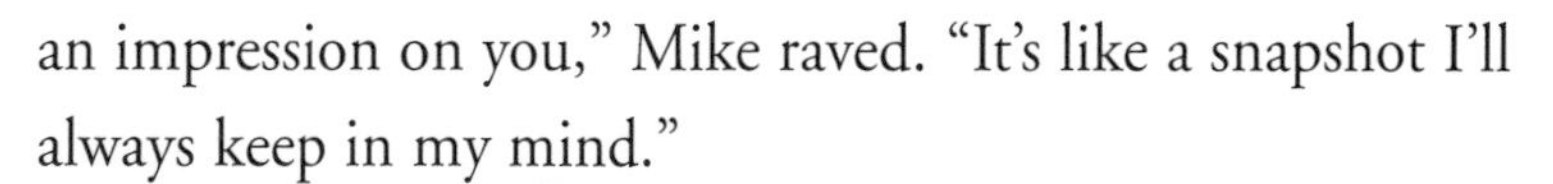

an impression on you," Mike raved. "It's like a snapshot I'll always keep in my mind."

Church Street between Vesey and Liberty Streets. ☎ (212) 435-4170. Tickets available at 2 World Trade Center (mezzanine), ☎ (212) 323-2340.

Web Sites To Check Out

www.newyork.citysearch.com: This site is packed with information on arts and entertainment, recommended restaurants (from Afghan to Vietnamese), shopping, and living in New York. It is well organized and contains links to many external sites.

www.nycvisit.com: This is the Web site of the New York Convention and Visitors Bureau, with lots of information on what to do and where to stay. Includes an event finder to look up cultural events for the dates you're going to be in the city. Also, offers publications including *The Official NYC Guide* and *The Official NYC Travel Planner.* The bureau can also be visited at 810 7th Avenue between 52nd and 53rd Streets. Telephone (212) 484-1222 Monday–Friday, 8:30 a.m.–6 p.m. EST and Saturday–Sunday 9 a.m.–5 p.m. EST for personal assistance in planning your stay in New York.

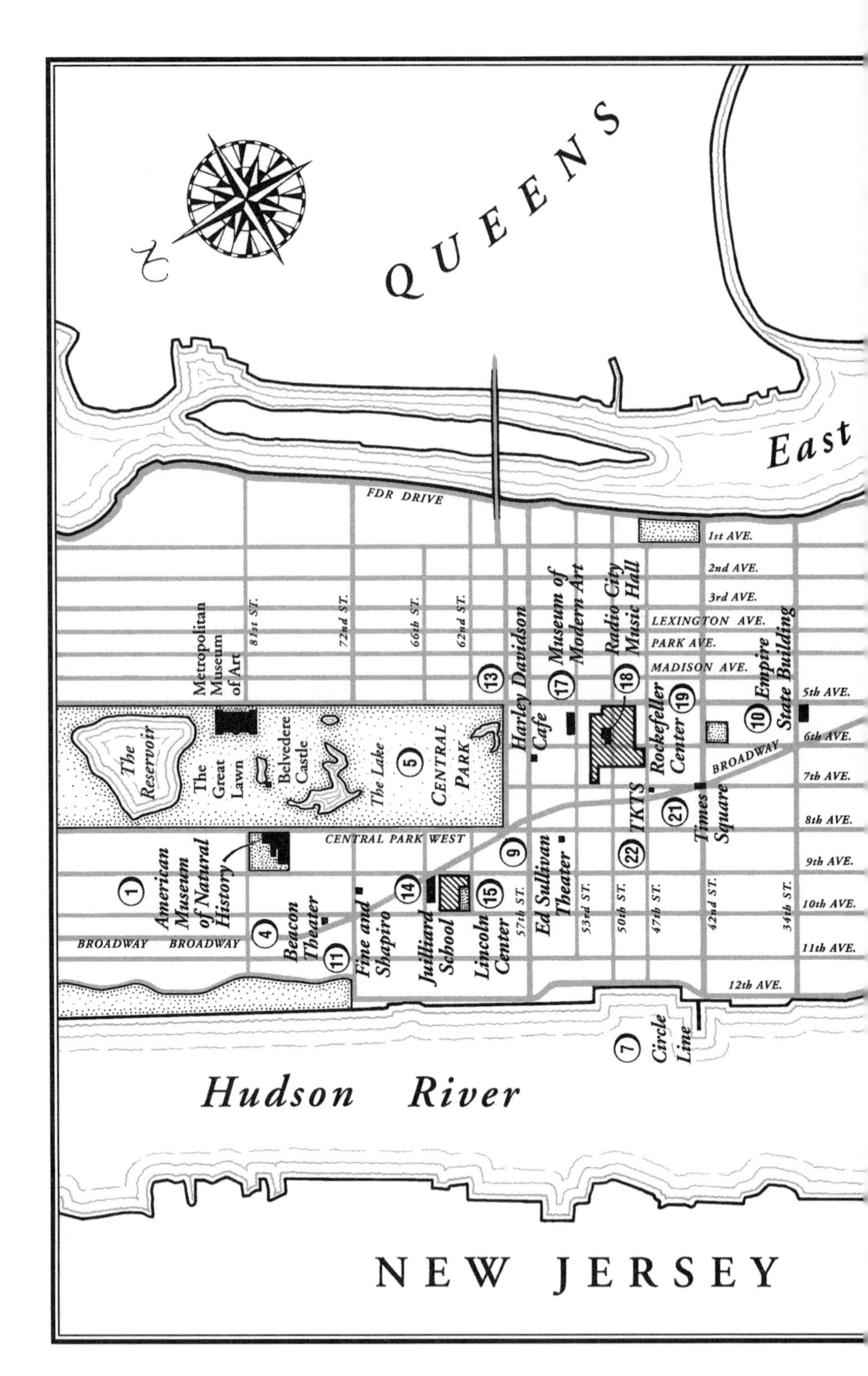
QUEENS
N
East
FDR DRIVE
Hudson River
NEW JERSEY
1st AVE.
2nd AVE.
3rd AVE.
LEXINGTON AVE.
PARK AVE.
MADISON AVE.
5th AVE.
6th AVE.
7th AVE.
8th AVE.
9th AVE.
10th AVE.
11th AVE.
12th AVE.
BROADWAY
CENTRAL PARK WEST
81st ST.
72nd ST.
66th ST.
62nd ST.
57th ST.
53rd ST.
50th ST.
47th ST.
42nd ST.
34th ST.
Metropolitan Museum of Art
The Reservoir
The Great Lawn
Belvedere Castle
The Lake
5 CENTRAL PARK
1 American Museum of Natural History
4
11 Beacon Theater
Fine and Shapiro
14 Juilliard School
15 Lincoln Center
9
Ed Sullivan Theater
13 Harley Davidson Cafe
17 Museum of Modern Art
18 Radio City Music Hall
19 Rockefeller Center
22 TKTS
21 Times Square
10 Empire State Building
7 Circle Line

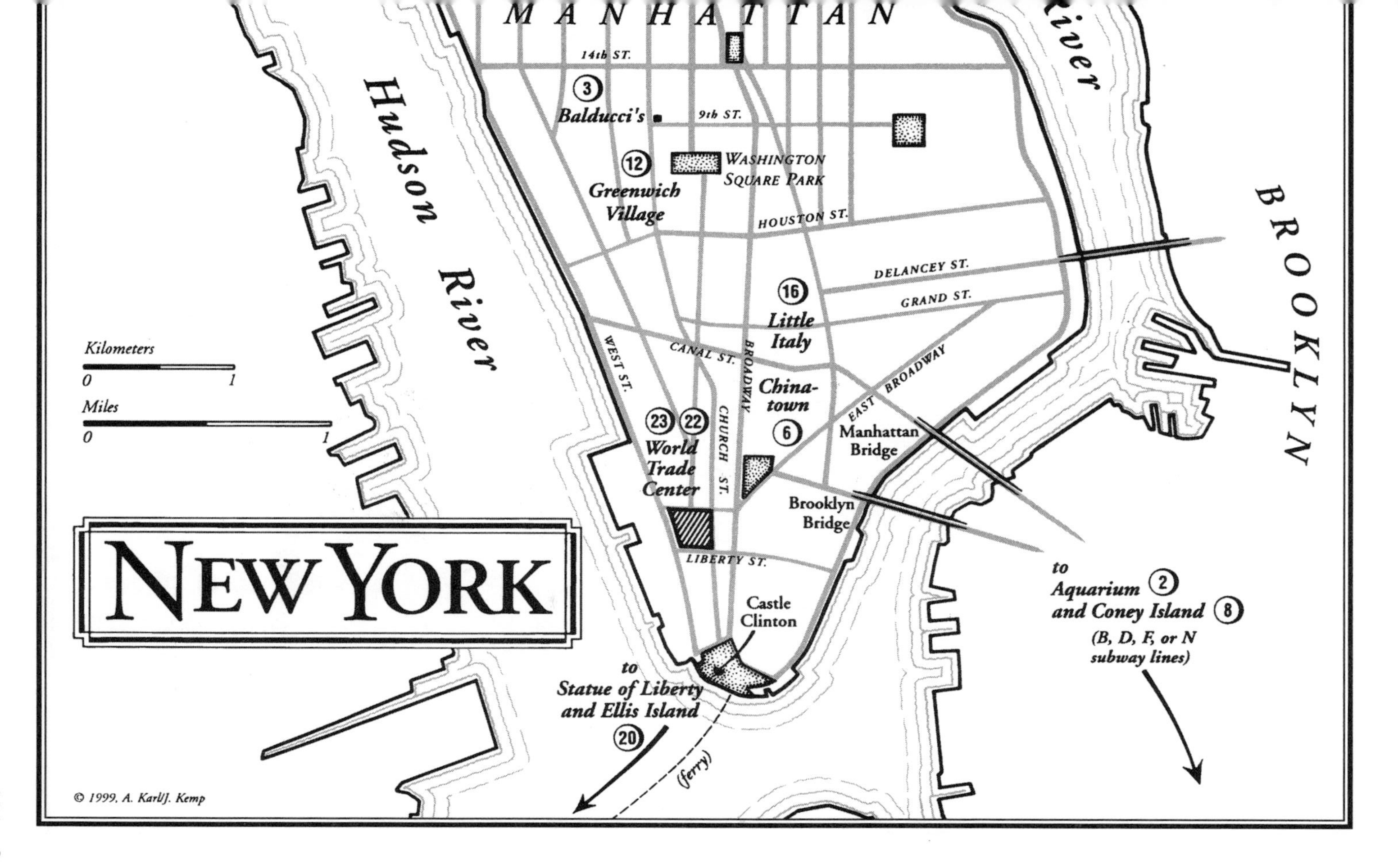

MANHATTAN
River
BROOKLYN
Hudson River
14th ST.
3 Balducci's
9th ST.
12 Greenwich Village
WASHINGTON SQUARE PARK
HOUSTON ST.
DELANCEY ST.
GRAND ST.
16 Little Italy
CANAL ST.
WEST ST.
BROADWAY
China-town 6
EAST BROADWAY
Manhattan Bridge
23 22 World Trade Center
CHURCH ST.
Brooklyn Bridge
LIBERTY ST.
Castle Clinton
Kilometers 0 1
Miles 0 1
NEW YORK
to Statue of Liberty and Ellis Island 20
(ferry)
to Aquarium 2 and Coney Island 8
(B, D, F, or N subway lines)
© 1999. A. Karl/J. Kemp

Also in the Going To series

The Bridges in London
Michele Sobel Spirn

The Bridges in Paris
Michele Sobel Spirn

Eliza and the Sacred Mountain
Virginia Bernard
(Mexico)

Eliza Down Under
Virginia Bernard
(Sydney)

Me, Minerva, and the Flying Car
E. R. Emmer
(Washington, D.C.)

This image of a monarch butterfly was chosen as a symbol for the Going To series because monarchs are strong flyers geared for travel. They migrate between warmer and cooler climates, often ranging over several thousand miles in a single trip.